"Hello, Carter."

The body behind the voice stepped into a pool of light, and Carter felt a ripple run up his back.

Kurt Richtor, hit man, originally out of Hamburg but didn't much care where he worked. He was big, mean, ugly, and deadly.

Carter's eyes flicked to Richtor's right arm. He knew that there was a finely balanced and razor-sharp stiletto under that sleeve. He also knew that the man could spear a pinpoint at thirty feet.

Ten short paces separated them.

NICK CARTER IS IT!

FROM THE NICK CARTER
KILLMASTER SERIES

AFGHAN INTERCEPT	LAST FLIGHT TO MOSCOW
THE ALGARVE AFFAIR	THE LAST SAMURAI
THE ANDROPOV FILE	LAW OF THE LION
ARCTIC ABDUCTION	LETHAL PREY
ARMS OF VENGEANCE	THE MACAO MASSACRE
THE ASSASSIN CONVENTION	THE MASTER ASSASSIN
ASSIGNMENT RIO	THE MAYAN CONNECTION
THE BERLIN TARGET	MERCENARY MOUNTAIN
BLACK SEA BLOODBATH	MIDDLE EAST MASSACRE
BLOOD OF THE FALCON	NIGHT OF THE CONDOR
BLOOD OF THE SCIMITAR	NIGHT OF THE WARHEADS
BLOOD RAID	THE NORMANDY CODE
BLOOD ULTIMATUM	NORWEGIAN TYPHOON
BLOODTRAIL TO MECCA	OPERATION PETROGRAD
THE BLUE ICE AFFAIR	OPERATION SHARKBITE
BOLIVIAN HEAT	THE PARISIAN AFFAIR
THE BUDAPEST RUN	THE POSEIDON TARGET
CARIBBEAN COUP	PRESSURE POINT
CIRCLE OF SCORPIONS	PURSUIT OF THE EAGLE
CODE NAME COBRA	THE RANGOON MAN
COUNTDOWN TO ARMAGEDDON	THE REDOLMO AFFAIR
CROSSFIRE RED	REICH FOUR
THE CYCLOPS CONSPIRACY	RETREAT FOR DEATH
DAY OF THE ASSASSIN	RUBY RED DEATH
DAY OF THE MAHDI	THE SAMURAI KILL
THE DEADLY DIVA	SANCTION TO SLAUGHTER
THE DEATH DEALER	SAN JUAN INFERNO
DEATH HAND PLAY	THE SATAN TRAP
DEATH ISLAND	SIGN OF THE COBRA
DEATH ORBIT	SINGAPORE SLING
DEATH SQUAD	SLAUGHTER DAY
THE DEATH STAR AFFAIR	SOLAR MENACE
DEATHSTRIKE	THE STRONTIUM CODE
DEEP SEA DEATH	THE SUICIDE SEAT
DRAGONFIRE	TARGET RED STAR
THE DUBROVNIK MASSACRE	THE TARLOV CIPHER
EAST OF HELL	TERMS OF VENGEANCE
THE EXECUTION EXCHANGE	THE TERROR CODE
THE GOLDEN BULL	TERROR TIMES TWO
HELL-BOUND EXPRESS	THE CLOCK OF DEATH
HOLIDAY IN HELL	TRIPLE CROSS
HOLY WAR	TUNNEL FOR TRAITORS
HONG KONG HIT	TURKISH BLOODBATH
INVITATION TO DEATH	THE VENGEANCE GAME
ISLE OF BLOOD	WAR FROM THE CLOUDS
KILLING GAMES	WHITE DEATH
THE KILLING GROUND	THE YUKON TARGET
THE KOREAN KILL	ZERO HOUR STRIKE FORCE
THE KREMLIN KILL	

DRAGON SLAY

KILL MASTER

NICK CARTER

JOVE BOOKS, NEW YORK

KILLMASTER #261: DRAGON SLAY

A Jove Book/published by arrangement with
The Condé Nast Publications, Inc.

PRINTING HISTORY
Jove edition/May 1990

ISBN: 0-515-10312-8

Jove Books are published by The Berkley Publishing Group,
200 Madison Avenue, New York, New York 10016.
The name "JOVE" and the "J" logo
are trademarks belonging to Jove Publications, Inc.

PRINTED IN THE UNITED STATES OF AMERICA

10 9 8 7 6 5 4 3 2 1

*Dedicated to the men and women of the
Secret Services of the
United States of America*

ONE

The meal had been delicious. Sir William Bellingham sipped his brandy, sat back with a contented sigh, and admired the youthful goddess on the other side of the table.

She wore a full-length white gown with a deep, plunging neckline dropping almost to her waist. One side was slitted, revealing a tanned, firm, lovely leg. High, full breasts thrust against the shimmering fabric, each offering a glimpse of the beginnings of round, creamy softness. Her blond hair glistened like wheat in the sun, beautifully combed, the bottom curved under in an abbreviated pageboy. Her bright blue eyes met his gaze, cool, contained, almost haughty.

"You're staring, Sir William."

"Yes, I am, my dear. You are stunning."

Her name was Lorna. He didn't know her last name and he didn't care to learn it. She had once been a British Airways flight attendant. Now she worked somewhere in the House of Lords. One of Bellingham's aides had arranged the date when Sir William had informed him that he would like a bit of celebration that evening before driving back to Sussex and his wife.

The aide was a smart lad. He knew exactly what kind of "entertainment" his boss preferred: young, blond, leggy, and not too bright, with large, succulent breasts.

Sir William Bellingham controlled nearly eighty percent of the textiles and dyes in the United Kingdom. The reason for the celebration was the defeat in the House of Commons that day, by a large margin, of a bill that would have opened a new textile trade pact with China.

Sir William hated the bloody Chinese hordes almost as much as he hated their cheap textiles. For years, he had been a vocal opponent of anything that smelled of dealing with Beijing.

The defeat of the trade bill that afternoon was a triumph.

"Shall we go?" he asked.

"Anything your heart desires," she replied.

"Anything?" he asked with a smile.

"Anything."

Lorna felt her skin tingle when he left a fifty-pound tip. That was more money than most of her men were willing to spend on an entire evening, and then only if they were guaranteed sex afterward.

Sir William drove his own Rolls-Royce. He nuzzled her experimentally at all the red lights on the way to her apartment.

When they were driving into the underground garage to her flat, he put his hand on her knee and moved it up to the soft flesh of her thigh under her skirt.

Lorna didn't object.

She gave him encouragement by slipping closer to him and opening her knees. When he kissed her, she let him find her tongue.

"You'll come up for a nightcap?" she murmured.

"I'd love to."

Going up in the elevator, Sir William remembered the not-too-savory look of the neighborhood. "My Rolls will be all right in the garage, won't it?"

"Of course. We have a security guard that does a walk-through every hour." Lorna didn't add that at around two o'clock every morning the security guard always sneaked back into the boiler room and slept away the last five hours of his shift.

When they were in the apartment, she tenderly placed his expensive camel's-hair coat in a closet. He helped her off with her borrowed mink, and she prepared drinks.

During the second round, they got down to business.

He began to kiss her and stroke her hair. To Lorna's surprise, she felt herself beginning to turn on to him. Sir William Bellingham had a lot of years on him, but he was an ardent and skillful lover.

Thank God, she thought; it would be much easier adhering to the note she had received than she had supposed.

It had been slipped under her door when she had arrived home that afternoon.

Lorna, the typewritten page read, *this is to make sure Sir William has a long, quite entertaining evening. It would be fine if he didn't leave until dawn.*

There were five crisp one-hundred-pound notes enclosed in the envelope.

She had thought it odd that Thornton, Sir William's aide, hadn't simply told her and given her the money when he'd made the date.

But Lorna didn't worry about it, not when it came to five hundred pounds.

"Ohh, that feels good," she crooned, and returned

the favor by unzipping his fly and finding him with her hand. "Ohh, that feels even better."

Well, well, she thought to herself, *all the rumors about Sir William are true*.

"Let me undress you," he said.

He did it slowly, kissing each part of her as he bared it. When he finished, she did the same for him. When they were both naked, he pulled her hard against him, his erection rubbing a thigh. He had quickly compensated for the difference in their heights, moving Lorna onto her side so that he might get at her breasts easily. He spent a lot of time kissing and caressing various parts of her. She decided she was very ready; she wanted him at once.

"Ohh, darling, you're getting me hot. Let's put it in." She had read the line in a book somewhere and used it on occasion.

"All right," he croaked.

She seized him. "I want you so much."

He mounted her, beginning to move inside her almost at once, gently but strongly. She was almost gasping because it felt so good. He had a breast in one hand and caressed her behind with the other. His lips worked on the available nipple. Her legs embraced him, her feet in the air.

And then Lorna received quite a shock. She came *first*. She climaxed like a sex-starved bride, noisily, happily, snapping her hips to encourage him and bring his own orgasm.

When she finally had to stop long enough to catch her breath, she was covered with perspiration. It had been the first time she had made it ahead of the man, and she was enjoying that nice glowing feeling.

Suddenly Sir William himself howled. He arched his

back and exploded. When the spasms subsided, he fell across her and rolled to the side. She nuzzled against him, purring.

They lay quietly for almost an hour, then he started to roll off the bed.

"Where are you going, luv?"

"It's almost two in the morning, my dear. I really must be going."

She tugged him back to her. "I don't think you're entirely satisfied, Sir William. I know I'm not."

Sir William chuckled. "I don't have your youth, I'm afraid. Once a night . . ."

"Want to bet?" she cooed.

She glanced at the clock herself. Just past two. She hadn't even begun to make that five hundred.

"I'm afraid there's nothing you can do about it," he said, laughing.

Lorna smiled at him. She decided there wasn't a thing she wouldn't do if it would produce the desired result. "Where there's a will, there's a way. Let me work on it."

Her tongue and lips and fingers became very busy.

Just when she began to tire, and was considering a brief rest period, Bellingham began to moan and move wildly beneath her. She continued enthusiastically, until she was sure he was hooked. Then she patted him and padded to the bathroom, leaving him gasping.

"Lorna, my God . . ."

"Only be a minute, luv."

She was an expert. She took thirty minutes.

When Lorna returned, Bellingham was still on his back, on the bed, in the same state. He looked up at her with a pleading smile.

She had sponged her body and put on a shortie night-gown that hid nothing.

"You are a remarkable man, Sir William," she told him.

She resumed her task. He reached for her, just where the nightie ended. She sidestepped with practiced ease. He tried again, reaching for her thighs. She let him encircle them with his arm this time, and grinned down at him across his heaving chest.

"I want to do that to you."

She slipped away from his grasp and retrieved the mink coat. Carefully she spread it out, fur side up, on the floor, and wiggled her finger in his direction.

"Let's do it."

At the end of another two hours, they found themselves back on the sofa. Lorna was beat, but she had accomplished her purpose. The false gray of dawn was just creeping around the drapes.

She feigned sleep.

Minutes later, she heard Sir William groan himself to his feet. Out of one squinting eye she saw him gather his clothes and head for the bathroom. She heard the shower running, and then he emerged fully dressed.

Through the same barely open eye she watched him slip some bills under a perfume bottle on her vanity and let himself out of the flat.

The door had scarcely clicked shut behind him when Lorna was on her feet, hurrying across the room.

There were three one-hundred-pound notes on the vanity, and a scribbled note: *I want to see you again.*

She smiled. "Oh, you shall, dear man, you certainly shall," she whispered aloud as she immediately drifted off to a deep, dreamless sleep.

So deep was Lorna's sleep that she never felt the building shake, or heard the sound of the explosion when two pounds of C–4 explosive split the Rolls-Royce into two parts.

All of the explosive was under the driver's seat.

Sir William Bellingham was later identified through his dental charts.

His teeth were literally all that was left.

.

TWO

Christie Greer was an attractive woman, five feet nine, thirty-one years old, with long, thick, sandy-blond hair now pulled into a neat braid that began at the back of her head. She had the fine-boned face of a high-fashion model, but the kind of full figure that is never seen on the angular bodies in print advertising.

It was her figure and her look that preyed on her mind now as she entered Mimo's Pizza Parlor on the extreme edge of San Francisco's Chinatown.

Max, Christie's editor, was a male chauvinist pig. All he could think of was her breasts and her butt, while she was on top of one of the biggest stories she'd ever had.

"Right now it's circumstantial, Max, a little proof, a lot of innuendo. But I've got this seaman—"

"Honey," Max had interrupted, "this could get a little dangerous for a pretty girl like you."

While he said it, he ran his soft, sweaty palm up and down her arm. She paid no attention.

"This seaman says he can take me to their contact here in San Francisco. He's ready to talk."

"Christie, baby, you've already had one threat to lay

off this story. I mean, you're taking on the Chinese government here. They play rough.''

"Max, the Chinese government is sponsoring shipments of dope into this country by the boatload!''

"I think you ought to turn it over to a couple of the boys. They can go where you can't in this town.''

While saying this, his hand had strayed to her hip. She managed to avoid it and head for the door.

"No way,'' she'd hissed over her shoulder.

"Christie, that's an order.''

"Fuck you, Max.'' She'd slammed the door hard as she left his office.

She was still fuming as she remembered the encounter. Her concentration was interrupted by a thin youth with greasy hair and a bad complexion ambling up to her table. "Yeah?''

"Just coffee.''

"No coffee. It's too late to make a fresh pot. No pizza, either, oven's broke down.''

"Just a glass of wine then.''

"Red or white?'' His eyes floated as if he were stoned.

In this neighborhood, Christie thought, he probably was.

"Red will be fine.''

The boy ambled off toward the bar. Christie sat drumming her nails on the tabletop and wondering if Pogue would show up. He hadn't had a ship in four months. That meant he could use the four hundred dollars she had promised him to take her to Yang Lee.

She was pretty sure Pogue would appear.

She wasn't sure of Yang Lee. His was a new name. In all her nosing around so far, the name had never come up before. Pogue, of course, could be lying, but her gut reaction was that the man was telling her the truth. The information he had about moving dope out of Asia and into the United States through San Francisco was too accurate.

After several minutes, the boy came back with a water glass half full of an oil-slicked red wine. When he had gone, Christie took a sip. It tasted more like vinegar than wine. She pushed the glass away and lit a cigarette.

Twenty minutes later, the ferret-faced little creature named Pogue slipped in through the front door of the pizza parlor, glancing over his shoulder. When he saw Christie his lips jerked into a smile and he sidled over to her table.

"Makin' yourself at home?" He sat down and hitched his chair over next to hers. "Hope I didn't keep you waitin'."

"It's all right."

"Havin' a little wine, are ya? I believe I'll just join you in that."

Christie eased her chair away from the table. "You said you could tell me where to find Yang Lee."

"That's right, and so I can. Still and all, it couldn't hurt us to be a little bit sociable, could it?"

"If you don't mind, I'd rather we got right down to business."

The bony little man licked his lips. He stared down at Christie's bosom. "I get it, business before pleasure, eh?"

"If you don't mind."

"Sure, I understand. Later we can take our sweet time gettin' to know each other."

Christie studied the little man and decided he reminded her of a lizard because of the way his tongue flicked out over his bloodless lips. She felt she could handle him anytime he tried to get too familiar.

"We'll see," she murmured. "Right now I'm in a hurry to find Yang Lee."

"All right, first things first, as they say. Shall we go?"

"Couldn't you just tell me where he is? Then I could go and find him myself and come back here. There's no need to take up your time."

"Don't give it a thought, honey," he said with a smile. "There's nothin' in the world I'd rather be doin'. What's more, I wouldn't want to send you off alone. The place I have in mind ain't nowhere for a young lady to go by herself."

"Where is it?"

"Chinatown, deep in where there ain't but alleys. I'll take you there."

"What makes you so sure Yang Lee is there?"

The little ferret cackled. "Oh, he's there, all right. An' I'm sure he's dyin' to tell you what you want to know."

His smile was a leer, and for a moment Christie thought of calling the whole thing off. It was painfully obvious that this odious man was only interested in his four hundred dollars and the possible opportunity to pat her ass.

As if he were reading her mind, he held out his hand. "There is the matter of some juice."

She took two folded hundreds from her pocket that she had already extracted from her wallet. "Two now, two when I meet the man," she said in a flat voice.

Pogue looked down at the money with his watery eyes, and shook his head. "Damn bad way to treat good money," he moaned, and smoothed the wrinkled bills carefully before putting them in his pocket.

"It's all spendable," Christie retorted. "Let's go."

She listened carefully as Pogue gave directions to the

cab driver. She wanted to be able to find her way back out of this rabbit warren if something happened and she had to do it herself.

The trip took about fifteen minutes through tiny streets and even smaller back alleys. A light fog had begun to roll in from the bay. In another hour, she thought with a shiver, it would blanket the whole city. The street where the taxi stopped was even narrower and more poorly lit than the ones through which they had already passed.

Pogue stepped out of the cab first and stood on the sidewalk peering uneasily around him and bouncing from foot to foot, as if the only thing on his mind were relieving his bladder. Christie paid the driver and walked over to join him.

"Well, where's the place?" she asked impatiently.

Behind her, the taxi pulled away from the curb with a lurch and immediately disappeared around the corner.

"It's just up the street a bit. This way."

"What's wrong?" she asked, forcing her voice not to crack.

"Nothin', nothin'," the little man replied quickly. "It's tough down here. These Chink bastards as soon knife ya for a dollar as they'd spit. C'mon."

They had gone about half a block when three shadows detached themselves from the front of a building and ranged across the pavement in studied poses of casual insolence.

"Just keep walkin'," Pogue hissed. "Don't even look at 'em."

The fine hairs on the back of Christie's neck were bristling. "Who are they?"

"Young tongs . . . don't look at 'em!"

As the shadowy figures moved under the streetlamp, Christie could see the light reflected off the grease in the tar-black hair. There were three of them. They wore leather jackets, tight chino pants, and heavy boots that thudded ominously on the concrete with each step.

One of them stepped forward as they passed. "Well, what do we have here? What's good-lookin' stuff like you doin' down here with an old man like this?"

"We do you much better job, honey!" said a second in singsong English as he grabbed his crotch and pulled it toward her.

"We even let your old man watch while we do you, honey!" hooted the third.

Christie picked up her pace, pushing Pogue along with her shoulder. "How much further?"

"Three doors."

"Move it," she rasped.

A few doors down, Pogue turned into a run-down building. It was double-doored. Inside the second door was a terrible stink of old fish and stale cooking oil and urine.

"Uggh," Christie muttered, stifling the reflex to gag. "Where to now?"

"Up," Pogue said. "Fourth floor."

She followed him up three floors where he stopped suddenly.

"What's the matter?"

"Nothin'," he said, even more nervous. "I'll wait for ya here. He'll see ya alone. Just knock and go on in. He's expecting ya. It's Four-B."

Reluctantly, Christie mounted the last flight. The hallway was so dim she had to snap her lighter to find 4-B. She knocked lightly, and then harder.

"Mr. Lee?"

There was no answer. With a trembling hand she tried

the door and found it unlocked. She poked her head inside.

"Mr. Lee?"

It was pitch-dark. She found the light switch on the wall and flipped it.

Nothing happened.

Leaving the outer door open behind her, she flicked her lighter. It was a large room with a linoleum floor. The furniture was old and scarred, with springs coming through the upholstery.

There were two doors leading from the main room. The first was to a smelly kitchen. One glance and she went to the second door. Behind it she saw a cracked veneer dresser, an unmade bed, and a broken-down chair.

But Christie paid little attention to the furniture. Her eyes strained to see something that made her give a gasp that almost turned into a scream. She stifled it with her hand and flicked the lighter again.

She swallowed hard as she watched the body swing slowly in front of her, the arms above the head tied to the light fixture. She swallowed again and forced herself to move closer.

The man was about thirty, maybe older. He had been stabbed at least thirty times, mostly in nonvital places so he would live longer. There was a pool of blood on the wood floor beneath him.

Christie's face went pale and her hands grew sweaty, making the lighter slippery in her fingers. She spotted a candle on the dresser and lit it.

"Get hold of yourself," she said aloud. "There's a reason for this. You're getting close. Don't panic, don't run. Look around."

She took a pair of black wool gloves from her purse and pulled them on. Then, as distasteful as it was, she searched the body. She found the usual pocket rubble, along with a wallet and a passport. A Hong Kong driver's license and various cards in the wallet identified the man as Yang Lee, 111 Queens High Road, Hong Kong.

She pocketed the wallet and passport and started through the rooms. It took twenty minutes before she found anything. It was an identification card that had been slipped under the peeling veneer of the dresser.

It identified Yang Lee Yong as a major in the internal security force of the People's Republic of China.

Her heart jumped into her throat. Proof, she thought, but still not enough. But it was a direction, and she meant to follow it.

She put the card into her purse, killed the candle, and let herself out. She wiped the outer knob of the door with her gloved hands and practically ran down the stairs. Pogue had disappeared.

Coward, she thought, *you can just go to hell for your other two hundred*!

On the street, she headed for the brightest light. Two blocks along, the same three young Chinese hoods stepped from the mouth of an alley and blocked her path.

She planted her feet and spoke with as much confidence and authority as she could muster.

"I don't know what you thing you're doing, but I think you're going to be very surprised."

The youth who had done most of the talking before leaned forward and gave her a loose-lipped smile. His breath was like soured milk.

"You a hot one, ain't you, real fiery."

"Don't come any closer," Christie replied in a calm voice.

He paid no attention, his voice a hoarse laugh as he darted his hands forward in search of her breasts.

Christie dropped to one knee. At the same time, she reached between the wide-planted legs of the young man and grasped his testicles. With all her strength she squeezed them together like a pair of ripe plums, twisting at the same time.

The boy screamed like a hysterical woman and dropped heavily to his knees. His hands plucked wildly at Christie's fingers. When at last she released her grip, he rolled over on his side still writhing in agony.

His two comrades stared at him in shock for a moment, then moved to the attack themselves.

One was thin and wiry, the other short and stocky like a wrestler. They moved forward as one while Christie backed away. When she was at a wall, they split, one to each side to flank her.

"You gonna be sorry for that, lady," said the wiry one.

The wrestler type started to speak, but the words in his throat came out as a scream of pain.

Christie lashed out with the heel of her shoe. It was a shattering kick that smashed his right knee. Before he could even grip his knee, she had two handfuls of his long, greasy hair.

The sound of his face against the brick side of the building was not unlike the sound of a watermelon dropped on concrete from several feet.

As the wrestler seeped into the sidewalk, the wiry one threw himself at Christie with a howl of anger.

She held her ground until the last second before stepping aside. As the boy slid past her, she whipped his face with both hands in a slapping motion. Back and forth went her hands, her body following the movement of his.

Her rings did their work.

When the boy turned to face her, blood flowed into his eyes from two deep gashes in his forehead. Two more gashes in his cheeks were deep enough to bare his teeth.

As he tried to paw the blood from his eyes in order to see, Christie stepped forward. She drop-kicked him in the crotch and then stepped aside as he fell on his face at her feet.

With a casual look around to make sure that all three of them would stay down, she walked away.

The crowd that had gathered a few feet away parted to let her pass.

"I loved kung fu movies when I was a little girl," she said lightly, in answer to the stunned expressions on their faces.

THREE

Harbour Park on the Kowloon side was quiet. The office crowds had gone home and the paths through the fountains and grass were largely empty.

It was a fine evening. The clouds had rolled back and stars had popped out in the sky above Hong Kong.

Nick Carter ran a finger under his collar as he walked under the gaudy arch and selected a bench directly over-looking the harbor. It was hot, and it would get hotter even though the sun had gone down.

He glanced at his watch, noted that he was five minutes early, and surveyed the harbor. It was crowded with vessels. There were Chinese sailing junks with their bam-boo-rigged sails, luxury cabin cruisers, sampans. There were some big ships moored farther out; an Australian aircraft carrier, an American cruiser, a British passenger liner. Little motor launches plied among them.

A step on the gravel path made Carter turn his head slightly. Strolling toward him was Peter Eston, MI6 li-aison with the Home Office, Hong Kong.

Carter suppressed a smile. Eston was right out of the Bengal Lancers: tall, leathery, marvelously British with a long aquiline face and clipped military mustache. He had a spectacular tan and wore a perfectly creased white suit. The rolled newspaper in his hand served as a swagger stick.

Like Carter, Eston took a quick survey of the harbor, the area of the park behind him, and sat on the far side of the bench.

Carter lit a cigarette. Eston unrolled his newspaper and looked at it, turning the pages from time to time as he spoke.

"You made proper good time, old man."

"You made Washington very nervous," Carter replied, watching an ancient crone rudder-propel a small craft across the water with amazing speed. "Are you sure the leak is ours?"

"Quite. The name is Ellen Quade." Eston paused as though he were bringing a file up before his eyes. "Born 1950, Valdosta, Georgia. Graduate University of Georgia, cum laude, master's in political science, Columbia University, 1973."

"Bright lady," Carter sighed.

"And ambitious. Joined your foreign service in 1974 and tried to sleep her way to the top."

" 'Tried'?" Carter said.

"She wasn't entirely successful. She tried to business-blackmail the wrong person, and got shuttled off to Bangkok for her trouble."

Carter was slightly vexed. "I suppose our people know all this?"

"Afraid not. Old boy network and all that. As you say, they all cover each other's hind parts. We were able to apply some pressure from a neutral zone, you might say."

Carter sighed. "Okay. What else?"

"Our little Ellen became quite pissed with her lot. Ambition turned to greed."

"In what way?"

"She is an extremely beautiful woman and quite well endowed, physically. She used these charms for profit. With her contacts through the embassy, it was quite easy."

"She became a high-class hooker," Carter growled.

Eston shrugged. "Let us say she accepted expensive presents for her favors."

Carter's face became slightly flushed. "How long has this been going on?"

"Give or take a few months," Eston said smugly, "about twelve years."

"Good God," Carter breathed.

"It is a bit of a sticky situation. That's why we alerted you. Thought you'd like to put your own house in order and all that, you know."

"I suppose I should say 'Thank you.'"

Another smug smile from Eston. "It would be the gentlemanly thing to do."

"Thank you."

"Quite welcome."

"Screw you," Carter said. "When did she turn, and to whom?"

"As near as we have been able to ascertain, about four years ago. It was about that time she was posted here, to Hong Kong. Needless to say, we haven't all the details, but we think it was the Chinese."

"How did they turn her?"

"The classic way," Eston replied. "Little gifts for idle tidbits of information she gleaned from her lovers. Once she was trapped, the gifts got larger and the exchanged information more important."

Carter flipped his cigarette toward the water and sat in silent contemplation. In five years the woman had probably passed a ton of British and American intelligence. That was water over the dam now; it couldn't be retrieved. Taking her into custody by the book and grilling her would do some good: What had she passed? Who was her contact? Had she subverted anyone else?

But that would take time.

Recently, Chinese agents had been on a rampage all over the world. There had been kidnappings, assassinations, and blackmail. Carter and several other agents had been working on it for a month. They had come up with zero.

If he could work up the chain through Ellen Quade, he might get to a man high enough in the pecking order of Chinese intelligence to find out why the agents of the Beijing government were suddenly running amok.

"You're very pensive, old chap."

"I'm figuring my moves," Carter said. "You've got surveillance on her?"

"Of course. She has a date tonight with a very rich, very influential gentleman from your Silicon Valley. He's in Hong Kong selling his wares. He is also very married."

"So, after she beds him, she'll squeeze him," Carter hissed.

Eston nodded. "Most likely, if he doesn't want to come back to a home sans wife and kiddies. His name is Harper."

"I would appreciate it if you would have a little talk with him and tell him the error of his ways."

"I'll do that," Eston said, "gladly. And you?"

"I'll arrange to take Ellen Quade into custody. But first I'll squeeze her a little myself."

"Admirable idea. You will, of course, pass on anything you learn relevant to our team?"

"I will, Eston. Where do I find her?"

"She has a flat on Garden Road near the U.S. consulate, number One-fifteen. It's the top flat, very posh. Anything else?"

"Yeah," Carter growled. "How did you get on to her?"

When a full minute had dragged by and no answer was forthcoming, Carter turned on the bench to face the other man for the first time.

"I get the feeling," Carter said, "that the uncovering of this female superspy didn't come from brilliant investigation and deductive reasoning, Eston. Why is that?"

Eston's stiff-backed, glacial reserve crumbled a bit and much of his smugness disappeared.

"Well?" Carter pressed.

"Well, to tell you the truth . . . we got a tip."

"From whom?"

"Don't know." Eston fidgeted. "It was an anonymous call."

Carter returned his gaze to the water. "Shaky. She's gone five years without a ripple, and suddenly she's flipped with one lousy telephone call?"

Eston stammered. "The caller had the facts. We checked, and one thing led to another."

"It smells," Carter growled, "but I have no choice but to check it out."

Eston looked relieved. He folded his newspaper and stood. "Then, if that's all . . ."

"That's all, for now."

The Brit walked stiffly away. Carter remained on the bench until Eston was out of sight, and then moved off

himself. He passed Queen's Terminal and on to the Star
Ferry.

The ferry was just pulling in. It would be about fifteen
minutes before it left for the Hong Kong side. Carter
used the time to make a phone call.

"Amalgamated Press and Wire Services," came a
pert, singsong voice.

"Leroy Hutchins, please."

"Whom shall I say is calling?"

"N3. Priority red."

"Yes, sir."

The station chief for Amalgamated Press and Wire
Services, Hong Kong—read AXE—was on the line in
ten seconds.

"Jesus, Nick, I didn't even know you were in town."

"I'm not supposed to be. Got a computer handy?"

"Of course."

"Bring up a schedule K."

"Got it."

"Okay," Carter said. "It's been intelligence out of
Hong Kong that's had me hopping for the last few
weeks."

"I can see that," Hutchins said. "Informer in Manila
on rebel arms deal, assassination rumor in Bangkok, and
a lead on Chinese bomber in Singapore."

"Right," Carter said, "all bullshit, nothing. I get the
feeling I've been led by the nose right into Hong Kong
harbor. Gimme the source."

"One minute . . . got it. Shan Lee. She's a dancer at
the Panda Club."

Carter smiled. "She was the source for all three tips?"

"Sure was. It's odd, Nick. She's been good. Worked
with us—"

"I know how long she's worked with us. I recruited her. Put me on tape."

When he heard the proper clicks, Carter relayed the entire meeting with Peter Eston, along with his own thoughts. Hutchins came back on when Carter paused.

"Christ, Nick, hot stuff."

"Very. I'm going to work her first. I'll call you when I want the CIA boys to step in and take over."

"Good enough. What's with this hopping you across the Pacific to Hong Kong?"

"I hope to find that out at the Panda Club."

Carter hung up and trotted toward the ferry.

FOUR

The Panda Club wasn't much different from a hundred others in Hong Kong—a lot of brass, a little flash, and very little substance.

It was early, so the crowd was light, mostly suits and briefcases having a drink or two and a gawk at the bare breasts before toddling on home to the wife.

Carter shouldered his way to the bar and ordered a Chivas, neat. "What time do the shows start?"

"About an hour," the barman replied, "but they don't really start taking it off until about nine."

"But the featured dancers are here, aren't they?"

The man shrugged. "Yeah, they're usually here by now."

Carter already knew that. He slid a twenty across the bar. "Tell Shan Lee that an old admirer would like her to join him for a drink."

"Would the old admirer have a name?"

"Nick."

The man faded through a door at the end of the bar. Carter sipped his drink until he returned, sadness in his eyes.

27

"Lady says she doesn't know a Nick."

The twenty came back Carter's way. The Killmaster shoved it back and headed down the bar. At the door, the barman blocked his way.

"I'm sorry. The lady says she doesn't know you."

Two more big bills didn't move him aside, so Carter stepped in close until the barman had to look straight up to see him.

"It wasn't your fault that I shoved my way past you, so why don't you just accept your profit and the inevitable."

The man started a swing into Carter's gut. It was blocked easily. Carter closed his huge hand over the smaller man's wrist, the thumb bent so that the knuckle would bite painfully into the softness between bone and tendon.

A strangled oath came out of the man's mouth and he waved a flagging hand toward the door behind him. "I suppose you know the way."

"I suppose I do." Carter shoved another bill into the partially paralyzed hand, and went through the door into a dingy hall. There were five doors, two on each side and one at the end. The first room was empty. At the second and third he said, "Sorry," and moved on.

The fourth was Shan Lee.

She was standing in the middle of the room, being fussed over by a pair of twittering girls in the act of dressing her. She was half in and half out of her street clothes. The top half was bare.

"Get out!" She spoke without making any attempt to cover the heavy, conical breasts that jutted impudently toward Carter's admiring eyes.

"We need to talk . . . now." The tone in his voice brooked no opposition.

She snapped her fingers. The girls gave up trying to cover their mistress's nudity and fled, one of them throwing an appreciative glance at the tall, glowering stranger in passing.

The door closed behind them and Carter took a chair, digging for his cigarette case. Alone, a little of Shan Lee's haughtiness diminished, but none of the cold anger left her eyes.

"Are you out of your bloody mind, coming here in person?" she snapped.

"Your accent is slipping, Shannon. Think of your image."

"Fuck my image. You're compromising me!"

"That may be, but I think you're already compromised."

A lot of the color went out of her olive face. Automatically, she accepted a proffered cigarette. He lit it for her and she, without bothering to find a robe, sat on the vanity stool at his knees.

"What's wrong?" she asked, much more subdued now.

"You've been taking money from us for passing along tidbits for how long?"

She thought a moment, expelling smoke from both nostrils and fingering the cigarette. "Three, four years."

"Four years, seven months," Carter retorted. "How much have you collected from the other side in that time?"

Her right arm whipped out like a striking snake, the sharp nails headed for Carter's face. He caught the wrist and twisted the arm so that her body lifted from the stool and came to a stop in his lap.

"How much?" he hissed.

"None," she gasped, "and I swear it. You should know better."

He stared deeply into her almond eyes for a full minute, nodded, and released her. "Yeah, I do."

She relaxed. "Then what's this crap all about?"

"You've passed us a lot of stuff . . . some good, some so-so. In the past few weeks, you passed three very hot potatoes—Manila, Bangkok, and Singapore. Remember?"

Her penciled brows furrowed in concentration and then she nodded. "Yeah, I remember."

"Tell me about it."

She had fairly good recall. Manila was an arms broker who had wined and dined her for two days and two nights. Singapore was an overheard conversation from another booth while she was holding off an American banker with twelve hands and a thin expense account. Bangkok was from one of the other girls who had been scared to death of her bed partner the night before, when he had waved a revolver around and told her that he was on his way the next morning to Thailand to make his fortune with it.

"Anything strike you as funny?" Carter asked.

She flushed with anger. "Hey, I do what you people ask me to. I listen, I pass on what I hear."

There was a knock on the door. "Half hour, Miss Lee."

She stood. "I've gotta get dressed."

Carter ignored it. "All three were bullshit, Shannon. The times you reported were perfect to draw me right across Southeast Asia to here, Hong Kong."

She shrugged, peeling her skirt and panties down over her full hips. "I don't really remember the dates. What's this all about?"

Carter watched until the dark curls at the base of her belly emerged, and then turned away. "Was my name ever mentioned?"

"Not that I can remember."

She moved to the vanity stool before the dressing table and sat. She had pulled on a robe but hadn't bothered to belt it. Both breasts were bare to the ruddy brown of their nipples. Through a cloud of cigarette haze, Carter decided that they were even more alluring partially covered.

"You're blown, Shannon. I think they used you to get a top agent into Hong Kong. Why, I don't know. Does the name Ellen Quade mean anything?"

"No."

Carter told her Eston's tale, and ended it with a direct order. "I think you'd better head back to San Francisco."

She whirled, fire in her eyes. "I would love to, if you bastards would give me back my passport."

Carter stood. "Call Hutchins on the hot-line number. He'll make all the arrangements."

Her eyes grew wide. "With the slate clean?"

Carter nodded. "With the slate clean. See you."

He kissed her forehead and started for the door.

"You're all still bastards," she hissed behind him.

"I know. It's part of the business."

Ellen Quade let the terry-cloth robe fall to the floor and studied her naked body with a professional eye. She saw a long-limbed beauty in superb physical condition. The belly was flat, smooth, from the puckered navel to the dark triangle below. The shoulders were wide, capable, and very feminine. If one looked very closely, one could see the toned muscles rippling under the creamy skin.

The breasts were high and well placed on a long torso that tapered to an impossibly narrow waist. The flared hips and smooth thighs were taut, firm. The elegant curves of the calves were made of muscle, not fat.

Ellen watched herself critically while she did a few simple exercises. Nothing quivered except the strawberry-tipped globes of her breasts, and those hardly at all. Now in her thirties, she was still as firm as a teenager.

Satisfied, she turned from the mirror. Her body was as efficient as a well-oiled machine. It would do exactly what it was called upon to do. And tonight she would call upon it to fatten her bank account by a good thousand dollars.

The robe slid to the floor as she moved from the bath into the bedroom. Humming, she stepped into a tea-colored pair of panties and put on a matching bra with a little bow in front. Over her shoulder she slung the strap of a portable hair dryer and connected the flexible hose to a flowered cap covering her curlers.

She didn't hear him enter the room. The hair dryer's humming deafened her. He was three steps inside before his bulk shadowed her peripheral vision.

Ellen looked up. "Who the hell are you?" she asked.

He lurched toward her. She tried to take a step backward. An oversize hand clamped on her arm.

She screamed. The other hand went over her mouth.

She beat at him with her free hand. It was like hitting a block of granite. The hand over her mouth tightened, digging steel-hard fingers into the hollows of both cheeks. Her head was forced back. It was impossible to move in that iron grip. The man let go of her arm and delicately removed the plastic dryer cap. His eyes roved over her curler-covered scalp.

She was making gobbling sounds, flailing at his chest. She freed one foot and brought a knee up into his groin. He didn't appear to notice.

"Quiet down, lady," he said. His voice sounded rusty.

She got her arms up high enough to start thumping his head and face with her fists. She whimpered.

The man dragged her over to the bed, his powerful hands fastened on her chin and arm. He flung her on her back, then knelt over her. The mattress sagged under his weight.

Some of the fear left Ellen's eyes. This was something she knew about. Let him have his way and maybe she could talk him into leaving without hurting her.

"You're Ellen Quade."

"Y-yes," she managed with a nod.

"You're a grade seven officer with the U.S. consulate here in Hong Kong, in charge of indigenous public relations and liaison with visiting dignitaries."

Her fear faded. He was going to rape her and he wasn't going to kill her. Those kind didn't talk that much first.

"Yes, I am. And who the hell are you?"

He grabbed a handful of rollers and yanked her face up until it was inches from his. "You don't know?"

"No!" she squealed.

"You've never seen a picture of this face? . . . You can't put a name to it?"

"You're crazy! Get your goddamned knee—"

"Listen, Ellen Quade, and listen good," he interrupted. "The party's over."

"I don't know what the hell—"

Again he interrupted. "For the past five years, you've been selling information to the Chinese Communists."

She wilted. Her muscles became rubber and the blood drained from her face. "Oh, my God."

He released her and walked into the opulent living room. In seconds he returned with a decanter of brandy and two glasses. When the glasses were full, one in a white-knuckled grip in her quivering hands, he flipped open his credentials case and held it before her eyes.

"That name mean anything to you?"

She read the top-level security stamp, scanned the name and the photograph, and looked up into his face. "No, nothing."

"Don't lie."

"I swear it. I've never heard of you."

Carter pocketed the case and lit a cigarette. "Who is your control?"

His calmer, lighter tone seemed to ease her fears. She raised her chin defiantly. "Am I under arrest?"

"No."

"I don't think you have any proof. If you did, I think I would be under arrest. I refuse to say anything."

"I didn't come here to arrest you. I came here to interrogate you. I want answers."

"Go to hell." She downed her brandy in one long swallow.

Carter crossed to her dresser. From a drawer he removed a pair of pantyhose and returned to her side. He sat on the bed and draped the pantyhose over his knee.

"There will be no arrest and no trial. I want answers. If I don't get them in one minute, I will strangle you and make it look like a robbery."

"My God, you're a barbarian!" Ellen cried.

"Not quite, but very close," came the calm reply. "You have fifty-three seconds."

"You wouldn't do such a thing!"

"I assure you, I can and I will. Forty-five seconds." He set his glass on the floor and rolled the legs of the pantyhose in his powerful hands.

Ellen was white with fear now, her whole body shaking. "If you're an agent of the State Department, it's inconceivable . . ."

"I am a very special agent. I do very special things. Thirty seconds."

She broke. Tears squeezed from her eyes and rolled down her cheeks. Her shoulders slumped and the glass fell from her fingers to the carpet.

"God, what a fool I've been."

"That goes without saying. Who is your control?"

She took a deep breath, exhaled with a long sigh, and turned to face him. "I only know him as Mr. Sek."

"Describe him." She did. Carter went through the Far Eastern agents he knew, and came up with a blank. "How do you make contact?"

"A floating restaurant in the harbor, the Serpent's Tail. I'm never to go there unless I need a meet. A waiter brings instructions with the check. It's never the same place twice."

"The meeting place?"

"Yes. It always changes."

"And if they want to see you?"

"I get a call or a note from my cleaners on Colby Road . . . my drapes or something are ready for pickup."

"When was the last time they sent for you?"

"About three months ago."

"Is that normal?"

She thought hard on this, blinked, and shook her head.

"No, not really. If I haven't reported with something, they usually send for me about every two weeks and give me a list of what information they're looking for."

"And they haven't summoned you in three months?"

"No."

"That figures."

"What do you mean?"

Carter ignored the question. "Do you always go to the Serpent's Tail alone?"

"No. If I have a date that night, I ask him to take me there. If that happens, I get my instructions from the attendant in the ladies' room."

"What's the name of the cleaners?"

"Loo Chi."

"At the Serpent's Tail, is it always the same waiter?"

"Yes."

"And the same ladies' room attendant?"

"Yes. What's going to happen to me?"

"That's hard to say. Get dressed. We're dining out. I have to make a telephone call."

Her voice stopped him at the door. "How did you find out?"

"You were dumped."

"What?" The surprise was real.

"I think your Chinese friends want to make contact with a top agent without going through channels. They used an informant of ours to get one moving in the Far East, and then dumped you in our laps to get him into Hong Kong at the right time."

"That's impossible!" she gasped.

"Think about it. You've had five clean, undetected years. Suddenly the Brits get a tip. They work on it and come up with you, a Yank. The Chinese dumped you, and probably a few others, to show goodwill. They did it through the Brits to rub our noses in it."

"Bastards! Those bastards!" Ellen hissed.

Carter shook his head as he moved to the phone in the living room.

It was always the most cunning and the most greedy ones who were the most naïve.

FIVE

The Serpent's Tail was in a triple-decked junk with a scarlet-and-gold superstructure shaped like a pagoda. The whole mess was lit up like a Christmas tree.

Ellen Quade had phoned from her flat, so a table was ready. It was only speculation on Carter's part that the owners of the restaurant, as well as the entire staff, were part of the game. But he had told Hutchins to correlate with MI6 and have the whole lot brought in upon their departure. He was sure that by the time they stepped from the water taxi to the landing of the restaurant, the cleaners would have already been raided.

The dining area was fairly full. Every male eye—Chinese and European alike—followed Ellen Quade's progress to the table.

She wore a sleeveless silk *cheongsam* so tight that it might have been sprayed on her body. It was shorter than usual, with a slit traveling all the way up her shapely hip. There was no question of wearing a bra under it, but the seamed bodice gave her some support.

"You do attract attention," Carter commented when the waiter had left with their drink order.

She flushed, but only slightly. "I didn't think. This is the way I usually dress on dates."

"Yes," Carter said dryly, "I suppose it's good for business."

She started to reply, but stopped herself and kept a thin-lipped silence as the drinks arrived and Carter ordered the meal.

They ate fried prawns and stuffed crab claws, Szechuan cabbage and meat dumplings, and finished with green tea, ice cream and coffee.

Halfway through his cigarette, Carter tapped her on the back of her hand with an index finger. "Don't you think it's time you made a trip to the ladies' room?"

Her eyes were pained as she nodded and stood. Moving away, she looked to Carter as though she were going to her execution.

Every male in the room again turned his head as she passed, the *cheongsam* outlining her spine down to the cleft in her buttocks.

In ten minutes she was back. Carter stood. She nodded.

"Let's go."

He dropped an ample amount of money on the table, and guided her by the elbow from the room.

When they reached the landing gate, Carter signaled the old sampan woman who had brought them out. Into Ellen's ear he uttered one word, "Where?"

"The Faiding. It's a coolie hotel near the harbor at Aberdeen."

"You're not dressed for that."

"I usually go back to my place and change, remember?"

Carter nodded. "I'll take care of it." He moved back to the old woman, told her their destination, got a price, and bartered her out of an extra pair of the tattered black pajamas and wide coolie hat she wore.

This done, the woman pushed off from the restaurant junk with a long bamboo pole, and started the ancient, one-horsepower outboard attached precariously to the stern.

Carter settled himself under the wicker canopy beside Ellen, and dropped the clothing in her lap.

"What's this?"

"Your new attire."

"But where do I change?"

"Right here, when we get to mid-harbor. What's the problem? I've already seen you practically naked, remember?"

"Damn you," she muttered, and then seemed to think of something more important. "You're not going in with me, are you? I mean, they would kill us both."

"In answer to your question," Carter replied, "no, I'm not. But I don't think we have much to worry about. I think they are expecting me."

Around the harbor at Aberdeen was a floating city of over four thousand junks and sampans. Over a hundred thousand souls lived, worked, raised families, and died there on craft that would never survive on the open sea.

Since the old sin-and-sex area of Wachau had been removed with the advent of modern high-rise apartment and office buildings, most of the petty crime, drugs, and prostitution had been driven to Aberdeen.

The closer they got to a pier, the closer together was the floating slum, a solid jam of hulls teeming with people. The old crone had shut off the outboard and was now poling them through a cleared traffic channel no more than ten feet wide.

Just to their right, Carter saw a matchstick craft that couldn't have been more than sixteen feet long. A withered woman in a conical hat crouched aft, cooking rice over a charcoal brazier. There were six small naked children clambering over the deck.

Carter could see that it was only a jump from the matchstick boat to the deck of a larger junk. From there he could walk the decks of other junks all the way to shore.

"This is where I leave you," he said, rising.

Ellen glanced up. "What if I betray you?"

"I fully expect you to," he said with a smile, "whether you want to or not."

He dropped some bills in the sampan woman's hand and jumped to the child-infested craft. All of them were on him in an instant, begging for money. A few coins pacified them. The old woman cooking aft scarcely gave him a glance.

He moved across the decks of a dozen junks without a pause and with only a few glaring looks from their owners.

The last three to shore was another story. They were well lighted and gaily festooned with colored paper lanterns. The decks were alive with young girls. They were brothel boats.

It was immediately apparent that Carter was European, therefore rich. He was swarmed.

"Good time, mister? Head job, hand job . . ."

At the far rail of the second junk, a naked girl of about fourteen was demonstrating graphically by making an "O" of thumb and forefinger and jerking a finger of her other hand back and forth through it.

Carter returned her smile, shook his head, and darted around her to leap to the deck of the last junk.

"Cheap motherfucker!" the girl cried after him.

He dropped to a low, free-floating pier and darted a glance to his left. Ellen Quade was just stepping from the sampan.

Carter slowed his pace as he entered the rabbit warren of tiny alleys. Keeping the high ground as a beacon, he moved deeper into the town, making sure that with each step he was climbing. Soon the alleys became paths where two people could barely pass.

Because of the hour, this was rarely necessary. Now and then a beggar appeared in a doorway hoping for a last coin. Twice, groups of teen-age boys took hard looks at Carter's expensive suit. Both times his hard stare and bulk parted them so he could move through them without trouble.

Eventually, he gained the peak, found the right alley, and started down again. When he spotted the coolie hotel, he paused for a look-see.

Ellen would be inside by now, still partially ignorant of the role she was playing. She would be feeding Mr. Sek whatever information she had gleaned in the last week. Mr. Sek would listen intently and eventually pump her about her dinner companion.

She would play innocent, or gush her guts out. It was immaterial to Carter.

It was all a game.

He was sure they had been monitored all through dinner, and probably during the sampan ride as well. For all he knew he was being watched right now.

That was all right.

He branched off to an alley that ran behind the hotel. In no time he was dropping down a short embankment to the rear door. Inside, a white-stuccoed hallway ran to the tiny front lobby. A clerk—bald and toothless—sat behind the desk watching a flickering television set.

Carter got the man's scrawny neck in the crook of his arm. "The Anglo woman . . . what floor, what room?"

"Fifth floor," the little Chinese croaked.

"What room?"

"Only one room."

Carter rabbit-punched the side of his neck and the little man melted to the floor. The wooden stairwell creaked, making Carter smile. He might as well have shouted, "I'm coming!"

Each landing was dimly lit by a five-watt bulb. Stairs to the fifth floor narrowed, with a single solid door at the top.

He used his left hand on the door handle. It was old, the kind you pushed down to move a heavy bolt. And the bolt clattered.

The sound reverberated in the silence like the first solid toll of a poorly tempered bell.

The door groaned wide under his weight, and he crouched. His eyes, already accustomed to the dimness, took in the entire room at once. Years of living each moment as if it might be the last had given him the keen instincts of an animal, both predator and prey.

Now, nothing activated those senses.

It was a large room with a few squat round tables and large pillows strewn about the floor. The only light was another five-watt bulb from a modern desk lamp on one of the tables. Its shade cast enough light so that Carter could see the hands, arms, and chest of the man sitting behind it.

"Mr. Sek?"

"Quite. Lan Yi Sek, to be exact."

Carter moved forward; a breeze carried the faint odor of fish from the bowls on the table. Gently, he tilted the lamp.

He was short, fat, with a face like a teapot, and slits for eyes that were as cold and as black as anthracite. He was conservatively and expensively dressed in a dark suit with a gray shantung silk tie.

"Well, Mr. Sek," Carter said, "you got me here. Now, what's it all about?"

The thick lips parted in a smile. "Bravo. I told my people that by the time you left Bangkok you would be suspicious. Giving you the Quade woman was rather a test. You have passed it marvelously."

"Where is she?"

"As you Americans would say, she is on ice for the time being, until we conduct our business."

"Giving up a top double and most of her contact net is a lot for a little conversation," Carter countered.

"Not really. Our business is very important. Miss Quade's contributions over the years have never been great. Her loss will not be great. As for the people in the cleaners, and at the Serpent's Tail, they are hirelings. Again, no great loss."

Carter shrugged. "All right, you went to the trouble, I'm here, talk."

"I am afraid not," Sek replied evenly. "The business I speak of is far too important to be discussed by one as lowly as I. I am afraid we must make a short voyage."

Carter bristled. "No way..."

They came from every corner of the room, at least five of them. They had been dark blobs among the pillows; now they were one moving mass on the attack.

Carter felt his arms in a vise, his legs as well. He felt strong fingers at the base of his neck. His head was snapped forward.

"Sleep well, Mr. Carter," Sek said, and Carter felt something rake his neck on both sides of his ears.

Suddenly he was released, but nothing was working correctly. He staggered. His spine seemed to be turning to jelly. He tried to lift his arms, and realized that they were already lifted. But he couldn't locate his hands.

Insolently, a palm was shoved in his face and he wheeled across the room. The wall hit his hip . . . or his shoulder . . . he wasn't sure.

Then all of him hit the floor.

Carter's last rational thought was how stupid were the little games they all played.

Bright sunlight filtered across his face as he allowed one eye to blink open. It came from an open porthole. That, engine sounds, and a gentle rocking told him he was on a boat. Slowly, to keep it on his shoulders, he turned his head and checked the cabin.

"Good morning, Mr. Carter."

It was Sek, sitting behind a low table, pouring tea. There were two Chinese by the door watching Carter impassively. They were both short, but stocky, with no fat. They were wearing dark blue sweaters and slacks, with gym shoes on their small feet. And whether purposely or otherwise, their sweaters were a size too small, emphasizing their bulging muscles.

"Where are we?" Carter croaked.

"About ten miles off the port of Swatow. We'll be docking in about an hour."

"And then?"

"And then we go overland, to Nanchang. I suggest you cooperate and enjoy the trip."

"Do I have any choice?" Carter growled.

"None," Sek replied humorlessly. "Would you care for some breakfast tea? It's English, very good."

SIX

Christie Greer stopped the cab when it reached Corn-
wall Road. She had the driver wait while she went
into a newsstand. She fumbled with her purse until
she found her address book and then the number of
Rhoda Carlisle. She wasn't at all sure Rhoda would
welcome this call. In years past, the two women had
been bitter enemies when it came to a story. But Christie was desperate. She needed answers and contacts,
and Rhoda's three years on the Hong Kong beat for
AP was just the kind of help—fast help—she had to
have.

The phone rang quite a while before it was answered,
with Christie growing more nervous by the second.

"Carlisle here."

"Rhoda, this is Christie Greer."

"Who?"

"Christie—"

"I heard you. Where are you?"

"In Hong Kong."

"Oh." Long pause and then a deep sigh. "You came
to town on holiday with no reservation and the Inter-

49

national Brotherhood of Christians and Jews is in town for a convention, right?''

"Not exactly, Rhoda, dear. I'm on assignment."

A low, throaty chuckle. "That ain't exactly how I heard it, sweetie. You were canned."

"News travels fast," Christie replied dryly. "I need some help."

"Always willing to lend an out-of-work enemy some money, honey."

"Rhoda, can we talk?"

"I was in the shower when you called. I'm standing here starkers, dripping."

"Does that mean go to hell, or can I come over?"

"Come on over," Rhoda said. "I'm going to hang up now before this puddle gets any bigger."

Christie was back in the cab in ten seconds and rang Rhoda's bell in less than fifteen minutes. She had stopped at another small store on the way to buy some Danish beer. She knew Rhoda swilled Danish beer.

Rhoda was waiting, holding the apartment door open. "Oh, dearie, are you on the scent. I can tell from that wide-eyed look. Come in."

She accepted the beer and put it away in the refrigerator, with Christie tagging along after her.

"All right, what's on your mind that's so important and what the hell makes you think I'd be willing to help you?"

"Bitch to bitch," Christie said, and grinned, "hope springs eternal."

She took a seat and cased her old adversary and her lair. Rhoda wore tight jeans and a man's white shirt unbuttoned at the throat and with the tails tied around her bare midriff. She was barefoot and her hair was a mess.

Still, Christie thought, the bitch was beautiful.

She noticed that the apartment was not very homey. There were no visible feminine nesting touches . . . the little things you usually notice if a woman occupies a place for more than a few weeks. The living room was as impersonal as the hotel room Christie had checked into less than an hour before.

"Nice place."

Rhoda's squawk passed for a laugh. "Don't give me that shit, honey. It's a place where I sleep and once in a while get laid when the urge comes on. Otherwise it's a dump. Now, what's your problem?"

"I have two months on a story, a big one."

"Yeah."

"I have two names and an address."

Rhoda exploded from the couch and crossed to the refrigerator. She grabbed two beers and returned. In the process, she talked. Loudly. "What is this? You want me to play twenty questions or something? What have you got, honey, and what do you want me to do with it, and what's in it for me?"

Christie hesitated. "I need you to run names down for me, and then run down any connecting names with the first two. Also, I need you to name me any high-level Chinese contacts that I can get close to here in Hong Kong."

Rhoda shrugged. "There are a hell of a lot of those. Did you forget the original question?"

Again Christie hesitated, this time quite a bit longer. Rhoda Carlisle was a viper and a vulture. Nothing would get in her way when it came to a big story. But Christie had no choice. She was out of her element in Hong Kong, and she was without any official backing. Also, she had a hunch that time was of the essence.

"I want your word that, when we get all the facts, I get a byline."

"Christie, honey, you're a big girl. We've been at each other's throats for years. I wouldn't give a byline to my own mother!"

"For this story you would."

Something in Christie's tone gave the other woman pause. Christie Greer didn't chase wild geese. If she said she had a Pulitzer by the tail, chances were she did.

"Okay, you got my ear, kid. If it's really that hot, you got your byline."

Christie sighed with relief, popped the tab on the can of beer, and began to talk. "Two nights ago in San Francisco, I found a body . . ."

Across the street and four doors down, in the same small store where Christie Greer had purchased the beer, a tall, slender, elegant Chinese man watched the entrance to Rhoda Carlisle's building while he dialed the telephone.

"Yes?"

"This is Ki. Dr. Sim, please."

"One moment."

The man waited patiently, now and then running his hand over his high forehead to pat his carefully coiffed black hair.

"Yes, Ki, I am here."

"The Greer woman perseveres, Doctor. She seeks help from another newswoman."

"Good, good. Our friends to the north have cleaned out Lee's apartment on Queen's High Road?"

"Yes, early this morning. His office as well. All trace of him is gone."

"To be expected. They are quite thorough, of course,

if a trifle slow. You will pay a visit to both places and leave a little more of the trail for Miss Greer.''

''It has already been done, Doctor.''

''And Sir Emery Duncan?''

''He arrives tomorrow at ten,'' the tall man replied. ''The reception has been taken care of.''

''Excellent. I am flying out this afternoon to the island. Relay your results the usual way.''

''I will, Doctor.''

The line went dead. The tall man named Ki bought a pack of cigarettes and exited into the sunlight. With a last look and a smile toward the door of the apartment house, he waved down a cab.

''The U.S. consulate, please,'' he said, and settled back into the seat.

SEVEN

The long black Zil turned off the main road and crunched along a graveled track beneath an avenue of huge trees. The road lay under a thick carpet of dead leaves and they crackled beneath the wheels, making Carter's teeth ache.

"Whoever I'm meeting, he must have clout."

There were three others in the car besides himself: a driver and two cloned guards. For the last hundred and twenty miles, none of them had said a word. They didn't break their silence now.

The big car came to a stop at the rusting iron gates of a walled estate. Both gate and walls were overrun by wildly growing vegetation. When the gates were open and the car was moving again, Carter could see the house about a hundred yards farther up the drive. He read it in an instant.

Mansions like this were all over China. They had been built and lived in for generations by rich merchants, the Taipans, before the revolution and the Nationalists' flight to Formosa.

This had once been one of the grander estates. Even

now, going to seed, traces of its former grandeur remained: the wildly curved, peaked eaves, trimmed in vermilion and black, elaborately carved portals still retaining their flakes of gilded lead. There was a tiled roof faded to a raw but delicate pink. There were a few fountains, waterless and overgrown with thick weeds.

"Out," said one of the black-clad clones, and Carter stepped from the car. He was barely clear of the door when the Zil roared away with its three occupants.

Free, he thought with a chuckle. *I can just run to my heart's content. Sure. Where?*

A girl appeared at the corner of the house and motioned to him. She was slim, with long, glossy black hair, high-breasted, and about eighteen. She was dressed all in black, with calf-high boots and a heavy belt fastened around her waist.

"This way, please," she said, and turned. Her English had a Cambridge or almost Oxford sturdiness to it.

They walked along a path choked with vines. Often Carter had to lift his hands to push back branches in order to pass. "There are no gardeners in the People's Republic?" he quipped.

Stone-faced, she pulled open a French door and Carter followed her inside.

The interior of the house had been designed with wide sweeps of space. The rooms were thirty to forty feet wide divided by screens of carved wood, embroidered silk, and translucent rice paper. The bare wooden floors rang hollowly under his feet.

She stopped at huge wooden doors fitted with brass rivets, and knocked. A guttural voice rasped, "Come in," and the girl moved away without a word. Carter stepped inside.

"Good afternoon, Mr. Carter. I assume I do not have

to introduce myself? I am sure my face is very familiar to you through your very up-to-date intelligence file.''

Oh, so true, Carter thought, as Lu Ty Yong, the top dog of the intelligence service of the People's Republic of China, stood and offered his hand.

Carter took it, and noticed the sturdy, Western-style grip. ''It would be foolish of me to say that I don't know who you are.''

Yong's face sported a cynical expression that was worn like a coat of lacquer. Carter felt that through the years it had become fixed. So much so that he could never change it. He was dressed in a beautifully cut Western-style black silk suit, white shirt, and gray tie. The whole of the ensemble pointed up the silver-gray hair he wore full at the sides. He was tall for a Chinese, solidly built, and Carter put his age at sixty, give or take a couple of years.

''Come, sit down. Tea, or brandy . . . or both?''

''Just brandy,'' Carter said, taking a high-backed chair near a low, black lacquer table.

''Sek tells me you saw through our little charade quite easily, yet you came in anyway.''

''Curiosity,'' Carter said, lighting a cigarette. ''Your English is impeccable. Princeton, wasn't it?''

The gray head nodded. ''Master's at MIT. We didn't really know what fish we would land with our little tidbits and the tip about the Quade woman. When we found out it would be you, I was, to say the least, overjoyed.''

Carter made a mock half-bow. ''My ego is properly inflated. Now, suppose you tell me just what the hell you reeled me in for.''

The laugh was a smooth cackle. ''Impatience, impatience, it is why you Americans get so much done yet have so many heart attacks. But you are quite right. It is best to get to the business at hand.''

The older man snapped his fingers. The beautiful young girl appeared from nowhere. The lights dimmed and the light went on in a slide projector. A second later, the slide of what looked to be a mini-massacre filled the screen.

''This was taken six months ago at one of the northern frontier posts. It was the result of a daring nighttime raid.''

Carter leaned far forward in his chair and squinted. ''But those dead border guards are Russian.''

''Indeed they are. And there was enough evidence left around to point to the perpetrators as a Chinese raiding party.''

''That probably raised some hell,'' Carter said.

''A great deal of hell, I assure you,'' Yong replied, not bothering to keep the bitterness out of his voice. ''It took intricate negotiating—and a rather large sum of money—to hush it up and keep the Russians happy.''

''I take it, then,'' Carter said, ''that the raiding party was not Chinese?''

''Oh, they were Chinese, all right. In fact, they were soldiers active in our army. They acted under orders, but the orders didn't come from their superiors. But more of that later. Next slide.''

A handsome, distinguished face filled the screen.

''Sir William Bellingham, textile and dye czar in the United Kingdom, staunch critic of the People's Republic of China. He was blown to pieces in his car on the night he successfully killed a trade bill in Parliament that was favorable to us. Nothing was proved, of course, but we were blamed for his death.''

''You didn't kill him?''

"We had nothing to do with it. Next slide."

For the next half hour, Carter was assaulted with the details of bombings, terrorist attacks, kidnappings, assassinations, schemes of political blackmail, and on and on. None of it could be laid at the feet of the Chinese government on the mainland, but all of it together was enough to sway public opinion around the world against the mainland Chinese and their leaders.

At last the show came to an end. The lights came up and the young girl freshened their drinks before leaving the room.

"What do you think?" Yong asked, sipping his brandy.

Carter took his time about answering. "If your people were not responsible for any of these acts, I'd say you have a well-financed, well-organized enemy that is trying to cut you off from the rest of the world, as well as putting you in place for a lot of small wars if it keeps up."

Yong nodded, and for the first time since Carter had entered the house his body seemed to sag with weariness.

"That is exactly the case. And to make matters much worse, there is not a great deal we can do about it without resorting to the same tactics. We have contemplated just that, but if there is even the slightest hint of failure and our people are discovered . . ."

He shrugged and Carter nodded. By this time the Killmaster had figured out what he was there for. "You want us to take the ball and run with it."

The cunning old face cracked a wide smile. "Not alone, of course. Let us say, we would like you to spearhead the operation, with the full backing of our complete worldwide network."

Carter laughed out loud. "That's a twist. You want

me to find—and, I assume, eliminate—the person or persons undermining your worldwide public relations so you don't get your already dirty hands dirtier than they have been in the past.''

"A rather crude way of putting it," Yong admitted, "but true. My country is finally stepping into the modern world. We have—or are negotiating—trade agreements with most of the West. The return of Hong Kong to us is going smoothly. Relations with the Soviet Union improve each day . . . or were, until all of this began."

"Father?"

It was the young girl again. Somehow, the fact that she was Yong's daughter didn't surprise Carter.

"Yes, my dear?"

"Dinner is served."

"Excellent. Come along, Mr. Carter, we will talk in detail better after a good meal."

Why, Carter thought, falling in step beside the old man, did he feel like he was in a country squire's cottage in Sussex or upstate Vermont?

The meal served on exquisite porcelain could not have been better if prepared at Maxim's. Jellied madrilène preceded a succulent roast rib of veal, accompanied by pencil-thin stalks of asparagus, and artichoke hearts garnished with fresh peas, celery, carrots, and tomatoes.

Each dish tasted as good as it looked, and by the time they had reached the fresh raspberry soufflé, Carter felt human again.

"An excellent meal."

"It was meant to be," Yong chuckled. "Had I served you fish and rice, you would have questioned my desire to recruit you. You see, I sincerely need your assistance in this matter, and will go to any lengths to achieve it."

Carter looked from Yong to his daughter. The girl's young-old eyes returned his stare unblinkingly. "You don't approve, do you," he murmured.

"No," she said, "I don't. I think my father has the power and the people to handle this situation without outside help, particularly American help."

Yong coughed. "As you can see, my daughter has a mind of her own. In most cases she is, even in her youth, quite astute. But in this matter we do not agree."

Carter laughed. "This entire thing is like a fairy tale, but if what you say is true, I'm sure my superiors in Washington would tell me to do what I can. What have you got?"

Yong moved his brandy and coffee aside, and opened a folder that had been sitting beside his place throughout the meal.

"For a long time, we were stymied. We could learn nothing about the higher levels of the organization that is seeking to discredit us. But in any undertaking of this size, one thing more than any other is absolutely essential. Money."

Here he paused, scanned a few sheets of paper from the folder, and raised his eyes back to Carter.

"For nearly two years, large amounts of currency have been laundered through Hong Kong and deposited in several banks in Singapore."

"Money from where?" Carter asked.

"Many places . . . right here in China, a great deal from Formosa, even Russia."

Carter frowned in concentration. "Why should that be suspicious? Money and profit know no frontiers. Your government and the Russians have long been selling gold quietly in Hong Kong, and using it to trade with the West in hard dollars."

"For business, yes," Yong agreed. "For buying and selling. But this money isn't moving. For a long time, it just sat. When it did start to move, in the form of withdrawals, those withdrawals coincided with each act of terrorism you just saw in the other room."

"Okay so far," Carter said, adding brandy to his glass. "In theory, you've got a connection. But where does it point?"

"That is what we must find out," Yong replied. "And three days ago, an agent of ours in San Francisco may have given us the key. The accounts in Singapore are controlled by one man. His name is Dr. Chiang Sim."

Carter racked his brain and came up empty. It showed on his face.

"No," Yong said, "you wouldn't know him. Dr. Sim is one of the wealthiest men in the Far East, but he keeps a very low profile. In the early days, he made a fortune manufacturing toys and useless gimcracks for the European market. Before the U.N. recognized the People's Republic and the United States backed off of Taiwan, Sim made a second fortune manufacturing small arms for the Nationalist army, with American aid. All of this was aboveboard and quite legal."

Carter got the drift. "And what did Dr. Sim do illegally and under the table?"

"He led the way in the manufacture of cheap imitations of brand-name clothing and leather goods. This had never been proven in court, but it is common knowledge. When that market began to wane, he switched to heroin. That isn't common knowledge, but our agent in San Francisco discovered it. Inadvertently, the dope smuggler was what led him to the Singapore accounts."

"Is this agent still in place?"

"No." It was the girl, and her voice was like ice.

"His name was Yang Lee Yong. He was a good agent and a good man. They killed him. Actually, they butchered him."

Carter glanced at Yong. "He was your son?"

The old man nodded. "Before they killed him, they purposely allowed him into the organization. It is my belief that eventually proof will surface that my son was an enemy agent and instrumental in smuggling dope into the United States."

"Another nail in the coffin," Carter sighed.

"Yes." Yong shoved a second file folder across the table. "Here is Dr. Sim's dossier. Please read it. When you have finished, join us on the terrace."

He followed his daughter from the room and Carter bent over the tome-length dossier.

It was quite a read. Sim had been in his teens when his father and mother had been killed by the advancing Red Army. Even at that young age, he had been wise enough to convert his father's cash—gleaned from the black market during World War II—into precious jewels and gold, before fleeing to Formosa.

On the island, Sim carried on his father's trade until he had amassed enough of a fortune to go into more legitimate business. One business led to another. Everything he touched turned to gold. It was suspected, but never proved, that much of his success could be attributed to a lack of competition. Many of his potential competitors just "disappeared."

Through the years, Sim was always radically anti-Communist, and had constantly advocated a return to the mainland. To that end, he had contributed a small fortune to small rebel bands inside China.

In the last few years, this had stopped. Sim had done an almost complete about-face. Now his efforts seemed to run toward keeping the status quo in China.

"Why? Carter wondered.

He closed the dossier and walked out onto the terrace. The old man sat in a wicker chair smoking a pipe and contemplating the overgrown gardens.

"What do you think, Mr. Carter?"

"I don't know what to think," Carter replied, "But then, the Asian mind has always mystified me."

Yong chuckled and waved to a chair at his side. Carter sat and lit a cigarette.

"Since the beginning of the revolution, there has been a secret inner society. They called themselves the Red Dragons. For years, they were very useful, especially to Mao. He used them to help foment his Cultural Revolution, which, as you know, set progress back many years."

"I've heard the rumors," Carter said, nodding. "There is such a society in Russia. They still advocate Stalin's hard line."

Yong turned in his chair to face Carter directly. "There is your answer."

Carter shook his head. "I don't get it."

"Let me put it this way. Old Marxist communism is not applicable in our modern world. The worst thing for a fanatic like Sim would be a softening of the old Mao/Stalinist line. A form of socialism with a slight mixture of capitalism would bring progress and economic stability. Without it, China and Russia would go backward. Eventually, they would wither."

"Another revolution," Carter said.

"Quite possibly. And if not, a bloodbath in both countries."

"Then Dr. Sim never really changed his line."

"Not at all. He is a patient and cunning man. In time,

he would have won. Even if he would not have been alive to see it, I rather imagine he would die happy knowing he had planted the seeds."

"And he has kept this Red Dragon society, and its counterparts in Russia, alive to that end?"

Yong nodded. "Youth. Through the years, he has planted well-indoctrinated young people all over the world, in positions in which they rise to some degree of power. Now I think the time has come for them to act in the West, as well as in Russia and here, in China."

Carter flipped his cigarette into the darkness and mulled this over before he spoke again. "How can he be stopped?"

"There is only one way. Sim himself must be eliminated. But not before the identities of his key men are discovered."

"And that's what you want me for?"

Yong leaned forward until his face was inches from Carter's. "There is a small island, Yatsu, off the southern tip of Formosa. We think that is Sim's headquarters. If you can get on that island, and inside his private domain, I believe you can solve all our problems with one thrust. Once Sim is gone and we know his key men, I can handle the dismantling of his organization."

"How nice," Carter murmured. "And how do I get off the island once I've done all this?"

Yong smiled. "My good fellow, that is why we needed a top-caliber agent such as yourself."

Carter lay on the bed, smoking listlessly. Around him were files, computer printouts, and assorted notes that he had made. The multitude of paperwork made up the problem, and the beginnings of a solution.

It was four o'clock in the morning and he had been at it for three hours.

There was a knock on the door.

"Yes?"

"It is me." It was the girl's voice.

"Come in."

She did, closing the door behind her and stopping at the foot of the bed. She wore a belted robe that stopped at midthigh.

"Well?" she said between thin lips.

"Well what?"

"Are you going to do it?"

The strain of her words had settled in her eyes.

"I got the feeling at dinner that you would prefer I didn't."

Her thick black hair had been coiled in two braids that hung down over her breasts nearly to her waist. Now she flipped her head and tossed the braids over her shoulders.

"I respect my father's desires and will do everything to help him achieve them."

"Bravo for you."

"Like all Americans, you are mindlessly sarcastic."

"Honey, you don't know shit about Americans. Now, will you get lost so I can get some sleep?"

Her hands began to move. She unbelted the robe and it slithered to the floor. Next came the bra, leaving only sheer black panties.

Carter stared. She had a good figure, everything well balanced, with nice legs and high breasts with brownish, protruding nipples on large areolas. She put the robe and the bra across a straight-backed chair, and turned to him, parading her body for him, yet still managing not to be crudely bold. She came to him, stood before him.

"What's this for?" Carter asked.

"I offer myself, if that will help you make your decision."

"Does your father know about this?"

"Of course not."

Carter slid off the bed. "You loved your brother, didn't you?"

It was the key. Throwing her open hands over her face to hide her tears, she dropped to her knees.

Carter took the robe from the chair, draped it over her shoulders, and pulled her to her feet. Gently, he kissed her forehead.

"Let's get some sleep, all right?"

"Kill him," she suddenly whispered. "Kill Sim for what he has done and is trying to do!"

Carter led her to the door.

"I fully intend to."

EIGHT

The shrill whistle of a tea kettle brought Christie Greer out of a sound sleep. It ended abruptly as she sat up wide-eyed.

Rhoda Carlisle emerged from the kitchen carrying a tray. "Good morning. How was the sofa?"

"Lumpy but wonderful. My God, what time is it?"

"Nearly noon," Rhoda replied, pouring tea. "I've been busy."

Christie was instantly awake and alert. "What have you found?"

"Your Yang Lee Yong was a real operator, and more. His flat has been canceled and cleaned out. His company is no more, and his office has been emptied."

"Damn," Christie sighed, sinking back into the sofa.

"Don't despair. We're still hot. Yang Lee Yong was a People's Republic agent, all right, and here's the kicker. His father is Lu Ty Yong, head of Chinese intelligence."

Christie was on her feet instantly, pacing. "Bingo!"

"His mistress and secretary was an East German refugee, defector, whatever, named Erica Gruber. Worked

69

for him for a year. She has disappeared or gone underground. I've got someone working on that.''

''But what about the dope connection?''

''We'll find out about that tonight,'' Rhoda replied. ''Right after we check out Yong's old office, we go see a sleazy little man named Koo Ling.''

''Who's he?''

''A smuggler who would sell his mother for a net profit.''

Sir Emery Duncan drove carefully through the heavy late-afternoon traffic. He was a powerfully built, big-boned man of average height, one of those types who put on a layer of tough pale skin during their early thirties and spread cushions over it later. He was about forty, his face broad and just going to flesh. The lips covering square white teeth were full. His pale blue eyes had developed a penetrating stare to a fine art.

At that moment his face was grim, the eyes slightly red. He had slept little on the long flight from London.

He swung the rented sedan into the dock area and came to a stop at one end of a warehouse, where a small but newish freighter with a Dutch flag was loading cargo. At the near end of the warehouse was a painted sign that read STANDARD SHIPPING LTD, WALLACE STANDARD, PROP.

An arrow pointing up gave directions, and Duncan entered a large, half-empty enclosure. A flight of wooden stairs attached to a near wall took him to the second floor. There was a short corridor at the top, and one door.

It was a bare-looking office furnished with some filing cabinets, a few chairs, a small desk, and a typewriter. Behind the desk was a cold-eyed, composed woman of about thirty. She glanced up as the door opened.

"You are the gentleman who just called?" she sing-songed.

Duncan nodded, and she indicated an open door with a silent jerk of her head.

The second office was almost as sparsely furnished as the first, except that the desk was enormous and there was a cracked leather settee and two extra chairs that had originally matched it.

The man who had been tipped back in his desk chair looking out the window past the freighter's superstructure glanced over his shoulder, took his feet off an open drawer, and swung himself around. The baggy suit, which fitted him nowhere, had once been white and was now yellow from countless washings, and the top half of his shirt was unbuttoned.

"It's very risky for you to come to Hong Kong, let alone come to my office."

Duncan glanced at the open door. Wallace Standard shrugged. "If she didn't know all of our business, she wouldn't be working for me. Talk."

"I have been informed by the government that my books will be audited at the end of the month."

"So?"

"I did some checking," Duncan continued. "The people doing the auditing are MI5."

Standard frowned. "That could be difficult."

"And that's not all. They were tipped off. My source tells me that they know about the Chinese connection."

"My dear Sir Emery, you have all the permits for importing into the U.K. from the People's Republic. If you have followed all the procedures that we set up, I am sure they will find nothing."

Sir Emery Duncan lost his composure. His face flushed red and he leaned far across the desk. "You said the pipeline was foolproof, there could be no leak! Well, now there is a leak . . .''

"Calm down, Sir Emery, calm down."

"When Sim brought me into this . . .''

Now Standard rose, the muscles in his neck bulging. "Sit down and listen! For three years you have accepted shipments of our heroin, and overseen the exchange of it for cocaine with your Sicilian source. Then, through your maritime brokerage company, transhipped the co-caine to the United States. May I remind you that those transactions have made you a very rich man?''

Duncan sputtered. Standard went on.

"We have discovered an informer."

"Who?"

"His name is Yang Lee. He has been eliminated."

Duncan's face went purple with rage. "Damn, man, what are you telling me? My last shipment was imported through this Yang Lee's company! His name is all over my files!''

"Don't jump to conclusions, Sir Emery. There is noth-ing to connect Yang Lee with our operation. In truth, he was an agent of the People's Republic.''

Duncan's fury turned to puzzlement. "Communist China? Why would they put someone under cover in our operation?''

Standard opened his arms in a shrug. "Who can tell what Beijing will dream up next? I suggest, Sir Emery, that you return to London and do a great deal of selective paper-shredding personally. I don't think it will be nec-essary, but . . .''

"Yes, yes, I will," Duncan said, rising nervously, the shirt beneath his jacket now heavily stained with sweat.

"Meanwhile," Standard smiled, "we will take care

of everything from this end, believe me."

Standard walked the nervous Englishman to the door. When Duncan had left, he turned to his secretary. "Get Ki on the private line. Tell him to proceed, but not until they are sure Duncan has phoned London."

"Are you sure he won't take your advice and go back to erase the Yang Lee connection himself?"

"Positive. He is too afraid, and he trusts his secretary implicitly. He'll have her do the shredding."

The name, YANG LEE: EXPORTS, had been hastily removed from the frosted pane in the door, but a shadowed outline of it remained.

Christie Greer flipped through a ring of keys, selected one, and probed the lock with the casual skill of a surgeon performing a routine operation. Two tiny clicks sounded and she withdrew the key. A solid metal shank was then inserted. Another click and the door opened without a sound.

The office was as cheerful as a Skid Row hotel room, despite the modern furniture and fittings. Everything was gray and tubular and functional. It looked just like what it was: a place for filling in time. Especially since it had recently been stripped bare.

In the center of the room was a long, bare, Formica-topped table and four chairs. Against a wall was a desk with a telephone on it and an ancient, high-backed tilting chair in front of it. Along another wall was a row of filing cabinets.

Christie flipped the light switch. Nothing. A small flashlight from her purse played around the room, her brows pushed together in concentration.

The police hadn't cleared the office out; Rhoda had

been sure of that. That would stand to reason, since they had probably not been contacted by the San Francisco police. Because she had taken Yang Lee Yong's identification, the stateside law was probably still trying to identify the body.

That left Yong's people. They would be thorough, making sure that they left nothing that would connect Yong and his dope trade with his superiors in mainland China.

But she had to search, just in case.

The file cabinets were empty. Ditto for the desk. She had expected as much.

She dug deeper . . . the toilet, anything taped under the furniture, behind the cheap prints on the walls.

Still nothing.

She was about to give up, when she noticed the leather inset on the top of the desk. One side wasn't even. It was slightly raised.

Carefully, Christie slid a nail file into the crack and lifted. It popped up and she peeled it back like the rind from an orange.

Under it she struck gold: detailed routes for the shipment of heroin from the Golden Triangle, through Hong Kong, to the United States and Great Britain. The receiver was Duncan Merchants Ltd, Regent Street, London

"Bingo!" she chortled, and headed for the door.

Maureen Kittering was tall, a tight black dress covering a long-legged body that rose up to large breasts pushing out with insistence. She had a young face, with a small nose and blue eyes, a pretty face that just avoided being hard, with hair carefully manufactured to a high-gloss blondness.

Now, as she replaced the telephone on its cradle, that face was contorted with pain and nearly white with fear.

Sir Emery Duncan's words rang in her ears: "Shred it, destroy everything!"

Her reply: "But the manifests . . . how will we explain them?"

"We'll worry about that when the time comes," he had growled. "Now, just destroy all traces of our ever doing business with Yang Lee Exports. Do it, Maureen!"

She walked like a zombie to the bar and poured three fingers of scotch into a glass. Her throat barely moved as she swallowed.

She had been Sir Emery's personal secretary and mistress for seven years. In that position, she knew all the secrets of his wealth and success, and she had shared in the rewards.

Was it over?

That thought, and the whiskey, jarred her into action. She snatched her purse from the bar, threw a light coat over her shoulders, and ran for the elevator.

On the street she hailed a cab and breathlessly gave the driver the Regent Street address.

Thirty minutes later she let herself into the office. So intent was she that she forgot to lock the door behind her.

The shredder was humming, and she had emptied the files of everything incriminating, when the two men stepped through the door.

"Miss Kittering?"

"Yes?"

He flipped open a credentials case. "My name is Collins, Special Branch . . ."

• • •

Sir Emery Duncan replaced the telephone and wiped the perspiration from his forehead.

His bags were packed. He had already paid his bill. He had confirmed space on the midnight flight.

On the street, the colored lights of Hong Kong were spread out below Victoria Peak. The dark waters of the harbor sparkled with lights as well, the lights of anchored ships and pleasure boats and the flickering lanterns of thousands of sampans.

Duncan paused. Should he even return to London? He had money in Switzerland and the Bahamas. Perhaps he should simply go to South America now. Maureen could join him later

No.

There was always Dr. Sim. Sim wouldn't like it if Duncan admitted guilt and ran. Standard had said that if the evidence of the connection were erased, everything would be all right.

Business as usual. And a very lucrative business it was.

Greed got the better of Sir Emery's common sense.

The rental car was parked two blocks from the hotel, where he had left it earlier. He slid behind the wheel and started the engine. As he moved down the hill on the winding road, a black pajama-clad figure on a motorbike fell in behind him.

Duncan drove slowly and carefully down the steep mountain road. Even so, the rider caught him by surprise.

Duncan had just rounded a curve when the rider whizzed by him and cut in too quickly.

"Damn you, fool, watch out!"

Duncan jammed on the brakes. The rider had miscalculated. The car grazed the rear of the bike with a fender.

The rider was flung to the ground, his motorbike careening off into a ditch.

Duncan emerged from the car howling curses at the young man who lay inert in the center of the road. Duncan bent over him. "Idiot," he hissed.

The young man raised himself on one elbow and grasped Duncan's necktie. At the same time, the other hand holding an ice pick moved in a swift arc.

The ice pick slid precisely between the cervical vertebrae and up into the brain. Duncan felt a sharp pain and a moment of intolerable pressure, then crumpled to the ground, dead.

The rider withdrew the ice pick. There was a single drop of blood at its tip. He produced a wad of cotton and wiped it off. He bent over Duncan's body and used the cotton to absorb the tiny drop of blood that had appeared in the back of Duncan's neck. Nothing showed now.

He then put the corpse behind the wheel of the car. The motor was still running. He put the car in gear and sent it down the mountain road. It would eventually hit something—an oncoming car or an obstacle at the side of the road. Perhaps the driver would be presumed to have had a heart attack. Perhaps not.

It didn't matter.

NINE

Yong's daughter was Carter's watchdog in the small plane south. During that time he found out that his original guesstimate of her age was far, far off. He had thought she was around seventeen, eighteen at the most. In fact she was twenty-eight, university educated in languages, and had been an integral part of her father's intelligence apparatus for six years. He also learned that she had a name: Myang.

So much, Carter thought, for first impressions when it came to Asians.

"Do we go back over through the New Territories?"

"No," she replied.

"Then where?" Carter asked with exasperation.

"Macao. It is safer."

So much, he thought, for getting information out of her. It was going to be hard to keep his word to her father. "My daughter is trained and reliable, Mr. Carter," the old man had said. "She will be around at all times. She will be my liaison with you, and my voice. I trust her to make decisions for me." Great. He had a helpmate who wouldn't talk to him.

It was still dark when they landed at a small airfield in the middle of nowhere. The transfer was made to a car in silence. In seconds they were once again heading south.

"How will you go after Sim?" It was the first time she had really expressed any interest in the how of it all since the previous night when he had ushered her from his room.

"I'll tell you the minute I know myself."

"Thank you."

The rest of the ride was in silence except for a few barked commands now and then to the driver.

They had no trouble with the Macao border crossing. On the Chinese side, Myang flashed a set of what must have been impressive credentials that made the sentries jump. They removed the barricade and saluted the car smartly as it passed through.

On the Portuguese side, money changed hands. Passage of the frontier in the taboo hours was clearly an established commercial business.

The bare, boring landscape gave way to oleander bushes in full flower, another barricade, well-tended trees, a shadowy stone archway, and bright lights in the distance. Soon the car was rolling on cobbles, and Carter knew they had crossed from China into the old Portugal of Macao.

They entered on the landward end of the peninsula. Traffic at that hour was almost nonexistent, so it was no time before they approached the waterfront area.

Myang turned to him. "Here is a number in Hong Kong where you can reach me at any time. We have given you the code name Dragon Slayer. I am Sword. Please use the names."

"How cute."

She paid no attention. "We will be monitoring you at all times, but it will be for your own safety. How can I reach you if there is an emergency?"

Carter gave her the hot-line number to Hutchins's office. "Just tell them it's a red communication to N3."

"How cute," she murmured, and reached across to open his door.

Carter had scarcely slid from the car before it was moving. He turned to the pier. The ferry was tied up next to a flashily decorated, brightly illuminated gambling barge. The barge was just closing up for the night and a dozen or so pedicab coolies squatted there, waiting for business to come down the gangplank.

From one of them, Carter found the location of a pay phone. He checked the ferry's first-run-of-the-day departure, and hit the phone.

"This is N3. Patch me through to Hutchins's home phone."

"Yes, sir."

Two minutes later, Hutchins's sleepy voice came on, fighting for alertness. "Where the hell have you been? I've had everybody I could spare chasing shadows from here to Singapore."

"You should have tried the Northern counties."

"What? You're kidding!"

"Would I lie?" Carter said. "I'll explain later. Look, Hutch, is the old safe house at Repulse still in action?"

"Oh, yeah, with all the gadgets in gear."

"Good, I'm going to need it. Also, I want information. Got a pencil?"

"Shoot."

For the next twenty minutes, Carter rattled off everything and everyone he thought he would need for an operation. He also asked for everything Hutchins and

Washington could get on the latest condition of several things and people.

"Think you can get someone over to my hotel and rescue my gear?"

"No problem," Hutchins replied. "Where are you now?"

"Macao. I should be in Hong Kong around nine."

"Want a car?"

"No, too showy. I'll cab it. See ya." Carter hung up and headed for the ferry.

Twenty minutes later, the ferry was chugging toward Hong Kong and Carter was concentrating over a roll and a cup of coffee.

He had formulated a plan. As much as possible, he wanted it to click without using any of Yong's people, particularly Myang. In fact, in light of the younger Yong's murder and the hell it would raise if and when it came out, he wanted no connection at all with the People's Republic.

"As yet," the elder Yong had said, "my son has not been identified. Why, I do not know. When he is, I can assume Dr. Sim has set up some unimpeachable way of connecting him to me and to the smuggling of narcotics."

Carter would do his best to head that off, of course, should it come. But the main thrust, and the quickest, must be against the good doctor himself.

By the time the skyline of Hong Kong took on shape and dimension, Carter had a complete list of people in his head who could be useful in the next few days.

People were moving toward the gangway. The cars hurrying along Connaught Road took on distinctive identity, and along the tops of the nearest buildings, the advertising signs blinked, moved, and shifted in a hectic panorama as the ferry, hooting hoarsely, headed in for the dock.

The clatter of the tiny bell made Rhoda Carlisle's teeth hurt as she moved into the shop. A thin man with a gaunt, hawkish face the pallor of a mushroom stepped through a pair of decrepit curtains and stared at her with bloodshot eyes.

"You want?"

"I must see Koo Ling."

"Koo Ling hard man to find. Goo'bye."

"Dammit, wait!" The man turned back to her with a leer on his cracked lips. "You know who I am. You've sent me to him before."

"Ah, yes, I seem to remember face." He rubbed his hands together and the leer got bigger. Rhoda placed a Hong Kong fifty on the bar. "Remember you very well now, missy."

"Where is he holed up?" Koo Ling never stayed in one place more than a week. As an informant, it behooved him to be hard to find. Everyone who looked for him had to go through one of his cohorts who also fenced for the thieves he employed.

"You wait."

He reappeared fifteen minutes later with a shifty-eyed youth who could have been his younger clone.

"Boy take you to Koo Ling."

Rhoda trailed her juvenile guide for nearly a half hour through the winding streets of the old town. The vegetable hawkers and the fish merchants were already out with their stalls smelling up the morning.

Finally the boy stopped in front of a decayed building that had probably been condemned twenty years earlier.

He pointed a bony finger—"There"—and held his hand out palm up.

Rhoda dropped a Hong Kong dollar into the palm. "Shit," the boy squawked and curled his fingers for more. She added a five and he bolted down an alley with a laugh.

Rhoda rapped on the door and waited. When there was no answer, she knocked harder and kicked it with her heel. Through a narrow slit in the heavy, faded curtains covering a single ground-floor window, a solitary eye was inspecting her. She ignored it and kicked the door again. A few moments later, the weathered, unpainted door opened.

The girl had a dark, pretty face topped by a tangle of silky black hair carelessly braided into two long ropes. The nose was full and straight for a Chinese, and the mouth soft, sultry and spoiled, with a cynical droop at the corners. She was wearing a cheap white sleeveless shirt that should have been washed a week before. It was tucked into a short black skirt. She looked sixteen except for the almond eyes staring at Rhoda brazenly. Those eyes had seen more than can happen to a girl in sixteen summers.

"I want to speak to Koo Ling."

"Why?"

"None of your damn business. Tell him I'm here. The shirtmaker called him."

The girl grinned and held out her hand, palm up.

"Jesus," Rhoda sighed, and jammed a ten into the hand.

The ten disappeared and the girl unblocked the door. Rhoda moved past her into a dark passage. There were three doors, two on each side and one at the far end, cracked with light coming through.

"Koo Ling?" she called.

"This way, Miss Carlisle."

She pushed the door open and walked into a room pungent with the smell of marijuana. She had to squint her eyes to see in the gloom. They finally adjusted to see Koo Ling seated on a fat pillow in one corner of the room. On a small black lacquer table in front of him was a bowl and an opium pipe. He was a small, shriveled creature, bald except for a queue of hair on the back of his head. His dark eyes were deep set over high cheekbones that made him look like a Mongol.

"Sit, sit, Miss Carlisle," he said, waving to a pillow across from him. "How may we both profit from meeting this day?"

"You've already profited," Rhoda declared dryly. "I assume you get a percentage of the fees it takes to get to you."

His laugh was a hoarse cackle. "Of course. But then life is hard, and expensive." Suddenly the smile left his face. "It is a busy day. What do you want?"

"Information."

"Of course. What?"

"There is a woman, German. Her name is Erica Gruber. She has disappeared. If she is still in Hong Kong, I want to know where she is."

"Very hard. Hong Kong full of people," he said, and shrugged.

Rhoda smiled through clenched teeth. "Koo Ling?"

"Yes?"

"Bullshit. Hong Kong is full of Chinese people. Erica Gruber is European."

"True," the little Chinese said. "I will see what I can do. Two hundred Chinese dollar."

"And something else. Gruber was the mistress of a

Chinese agent named Yang Lee Yong. Yang Lee was shipping opium paste or raw heroin . . .''

"Very dangerous, missy. Some things are better left unknown.''

From her purse Rhoda took five one-hundred-dollar bills and laid them on the table. "I never reveal my sources, Koo Ling, you know that. I think Yang Lee Yong's backing came from Beijing. You can find out. I need proof.''

Koo Ling eyed the money, then Rhoda's determined face. "Another five hundred Hong Kong if I am able to learn what you desire?''

"Agreed." Rhoda stood. "You have my office and my flat number. Speed is important.''

"I will do my best.''

Rhoda turned and left the room.

Koo Ling reached beneath the table and lifted a telephone. The other end answered on the first ring.

"Yes?''

"A Miss Rhoda Carlisle is also interested in the Gruber woman.''

"She is . . . ?''

"A reporter, Associated Press. She also wants information about Yang Lee Yong's recent activities . . .''

Rhoda breathed deeply when she got back on the street. Christie would have the lead and most of the story written by now. If they could get the rest of the pieces put together by that evening, they could take the whole package to her editor in the morning.

At a kiosk she bought the morning newspapers and then hailed a cab.

The cab was just pulling up to her building when Rhoda saw the brief story on page two: *U.K. businessman, Sir Emery Duncan, dies in motorcar accident.*

• • •

The apartment entrance was in the back off a small courtyard, merely an opening in the wall, with no concierge or nightwatchman. An apartment block of anonymous people in which everyone minded his own business, ignoring his neighbors. Carter went inside, and paused. The lobby was floored with concrete and dirty, littered with long-discarded cigarette butts, paper, and leaves. Above, he heard the murmur of activity from the apartments, like the humming of a beehive. Somewhere a radio blared music and a voice sounded loudly in an unintelligible argument. The smell of cooking permeated everywhere.

Carter found the rear stairs and descended to a steel door. In Chinese and English a hand-lettered sign read PERSONNEL ONLY—NO ADMITTANCE.

There was a buzzer hidden in the molding above the door. Carter jabbed it, three shorts and a long. There was a click and the door sagged open.

Beyond it was a short hallway ending in a wooden door. It was opened just as Carter reached it, and Leroy Hutchins greeted him.

"Welcome home."

"Thanks. You got my gear?"

"In there," Hutchins told him.

Carter moved through an office with two desks, telephones, a monster scrambling machine, and a high-speed teletype, into a sitting room. Through another door was a comfortable bedroom. On the bed his bags had been opened.

He started to strip off his clothing the moment he hit the room. "Talk to me."

Hutchins lounged against a wall and consulted a clipboard as he spoke. "They released Ellen Quade. Must have been right after they got you. We picked her up at her flat. She was getting ready to run.''

"Of course," Carter said. "Anything?"

"Nothing. She admitted everything, but didn't realize she was being suckered. We didn't get anything more of value out of her. She's being held now until this all blows over. Eventually, we'll cut her up. Nothing from the hired hands at the cleaners or the floating restaurant.''

"I didn't expect anything," Carter growled, moving into the bath and lathering his face for a shave. "What about Yong's info?"

"It all checks . . . times, places, the whole nine yards. Got the interrogation on Lorna Crue and Bellingham's aide in London. They were both suckered. All in all, old man Yong looks to be telling the truth. You going after this Dr. Sim?"

"No choice," Carter replied, rinsing the lather from his face. "You checked San Francisco?"

"Yep. The P.D. there was very happy to find out who their stiff was. They were more than happy to accommodate. Everything will be kept hush-hush until we give them the word to ship him back here.''

Carter was dressing—lightweight slacks, sport shirt, windbreaker, and the shoulder harness for Wilhelmina, his 9mm Luger. Hugo, his stiletto, went into a harness around his left ankle.

"What about the rest?"

"Lady Pi Pang will cooperate, but she wants to hear the whole deal directly from your golden lips."

"Figures," Carter smirked. "She also wants to make sure the fee is clearly understood. What about my cover?"

"I've contacted the consulate. A guy by the name of Kwon Ki handles this sort of thing for us. He's setting you up with papers, passport, visa, everything you'll need to get into Taiwan. Drop by the consulate when you leave here. Use the VIP rear entrance. Ask for Ki. He needs fresh photographs.''

"Will do," Carter said. "What am I?"

"You're a buyer for a West Coast discount chain. You're in the market for about a million dollars' worth of rip-off jeans, handbags, shoes, the lot.''

"I thought Sim was laying off that stuff.''

"He's always in the market for money, from anywhere," Hutchins replied. "For a million or more he'll gear up fast. The factories are on the island, so that should get you out there.''

Carter dropped a hand on the other man's shoulder. "Good job. I'll see if Lady Pang and company can get me off the island. Do I have wheels?''

Hutchins dropped a set of keys in Carter's hand. "A red Lotus.''

"Red?"

"Red," Hutchins said, and grinned. "It's the best I could do on short notice. We use it for posh jobs.''

Carter laughed. "I'll consider this one. We'll send the whole bill to Beijing anyway.''

He found the low-slung sports car in an alley behind the safe house. Conspicuous it was, but two times through the gears and Carter started enjoying the feeling of power.

What the hell, he thought, *us bad guys should go first class every once in a while.*

TEN

Carter rang the bell at the rear VIP entrance of the U.S. consulate. It was opened at once by a tired, gray-haired guardian in a morning suit.

"Yes, sir?"

Carter flashed his credentials. "I'm to see Kwon Ki."

"This way, sir."

Carter followed the old man through a maze of hallways and stairs until he ended up in front of a door somewhere on the fourth floor.

"Go right in, sir. You are expected."

The office was efficient, ordered, walled with file cabinets and swivel chairs. A small metal desk took up one side of the room. On the top, a tray held a neat stack of papers, and beside it, a file folder rested. It was an office that reflected the man behind the desk, his shirt fresh, smartly creased, his face even-featured and composed. It was a face with nothing to distinguish it from a thousand other faces, except possibly the eyes. They were dark and they held shrewdness mingled with grimness. They were eyes that had seen more of life than they had wanted to see.

91

He rose as Carter approached the desk and extended his hand almost reluctantly. "Mr. Carter?"

"Yes."

"I am Kwon Ki."

The physique was reedy but the grip was like steel. Carter had to squeeze hard to match the viselike pressure.

"I understand you have some papers for me."

"I am preparing papers, yes. Please, sit down."

Carter sat. Ki sat, and sipped from a cup of coffee. He made no effort to offer Carter a cup.

"You understand that this is very irregular. State does not like to do this sort of thing."

Carter could almost feel the heat of the other man's animosity toward him. "Mr. Ki, I am just another American who has lost his passport."

"Of course you are," Ki replied dryly. He pulled a form pad toward him and picked up a pen. He machine-gunned the required questions and Carter answered. "You will need only the Taiwan visa?"

"Just Taiwan."

Ki consulted a notepad. "You will be a representative of Orgon Discount Stores of California?"

"That's right, a buyer."

"And what is your reason for visiting Taiwan?"

"Is that necessary?"

Ki sighed. "It is. The government over there is very strict."

"Let's say I'll be trying to open up new purchasing markets."

Ki frowned and wrote. "Will you be traveling on Formosa?"

"None of your bloody business."

Ki froze, his dead eyes boring through Carter. "I see. Room Three-twelve, next floor down, for photographs."

Carter stood. "When will everything be ready?"

"Early tomorrow morning."

Carter nodded. "I'll have them picked up."

"And, Mr. Carter, should your activities in Taiwan be indiscreet, the consulate will have no record of the passport. Of course, I suppose you know that."

"Of course."

Carter turned away and headed for the third floor. *Bloody bureaucrat,* he thought.

The red light on the console was gleaming when Carter climbed back into the Lotus. He hit the play button on the tape, and Hutchins's voice came through the car speakers.

"Got a call on the red line, a woman, used the name Sword. She used your agency designation, so I assume you know about it. Says she needs a call from you post-haste and you have the number. Stay in touch."

"Shit," Carter groaned, and gunned the Lotus.

Halfway around the island, he stopped at a fish house and grabbed some lunch. When he had eaten, he bribed the owner to let him use the phone. He dialed the number Myang had given him, and a husky voice answered in Chinese.

"This is Car . . . uh, this is Dragon Slayer. Let me speak to Sword."

A grunt, and seconds later Myang came on the line. There were no hellos, she just dived in.

"Something very important has come up. I must see you at once."

"I have an appointment," Carter replied, "also very important. What's up?"

"I cannot speak on the phone. It is most urgent. You

are not far. I am at number Ten Foo Chow Mews in ShekeQ, just off the beach.''

"I'll be there in a couple of hours—"

"No, *now*," she insisted. "You are near Ocean Park. Shek-O is not far from there. I shall expect you within the hour.''

The line went dead before Carter could ask her how she knew so precisely where he was. And then he remembered her words in the car just before he had left her to take the ferry: "We will be monitoring you at all times, but it will be for your own safety.''

"Sure," Carter mumbled aloud, "my own safety.''

It wasn't hard to spot them in the small parking lot, two vacant eyes in each vacant, staring face. And they made no bones about staring at him as he walked to his car.

This should be a spot of fun, Carter thought, as he turned the key and the powerful Lotus roared to life. As he pulled from the parking lot, the little green Ford Fiesta slid in behind him.

The right-hand turn would take him to Repulse Bay and Lady Pang's villa. He took the left and started climbing inland, toward the hills.

He didn't push or try them at first. The Lotus felt fine and sounded good. The exhaust was a vigorous, healthy growl. Behind him, the Ford was keeping its distance. Carter gained speed. He hit sixty, then seventy. The curves shot past; he took them with tires squealing.

A quick glance told him that the Ford driver was game even though the compact had no hopes of cornering at the Lotus's high speeds.

He pushed the speedometer up to eighty. The curves grew tighter. He cut them, starting outside, slipping in toward the rock wall, then out again. The road was deserted.

Already the Ford was fading back.

The road curved gently downward. It was a good road. Carter hoped it wasn't the only one across the island's center.

He poured more gas to the twin carbs of the Lotus and the engine seemed to hum in appreciation. The road continued down, the curves growing sharper, the pavement narrower. He maintained his speed, the wind through the open window roaring wildly in his ears and tugging at his hair.

He was putting more and more distance between himself and the Ford with each second. He took another curve, and momentarily the smaller car was lost behind the bend.

The speedometer went up to one-ten. The engine was working hard now, screaming like a tortured demon with the wind. He took the next curve sloppily, bouncing from the rock face to the stone wall, then miraculously back to the center of the road.

It was close and dangerous, but he kept his foot down.

The road grew narrower still. That was good. Another curve coming up, a deadly one, sharp and blind. He slowed slightly, then slammed on his brakes.

The car skidded, the rear end spinning forward. He turned 180 degrees, then stopped, the motor dead. The Lotus was facing the Ford as the smaller car skidded around the curve.

Carter could see the silent screams erupting from the men as the driver stood on his own brakes and wrenched the wheel. He had little choice. He could go through the guardrail, directly into the Lotus, and possibly send both cars off the edge, or smash into the rock wall.

He chose the latter and there was a metal-grinding crash.

Carter put the Lotus in gear and edged around them with a wave and a smile.

Rhoda Carlisle slid into the bucket seat of her MG and started the engine with a grim smile on her face.

The police had been tight-lipped about Sir Emery Duncan, but Christie had cultivated a lot of the lower-echelon people who handled paperwork for the supervisors and detectives.

An autopsy revealed that Sir Emery had been dead when his car had careened over a cliff. Officially, as far as the press was concerned, it was still an accident. But off the record, they were opening a homicide investigation.

The "off-the-record" was fine with Rhoda. She had bigger fish to fry than Sir Emery Duncan's way of demise. What concerned her, and of course Christie Greer, was *why* Duncan had been killed, and what he was doing in Hong Kong.

When she also learned that an order had come through from MI5 in London to put a lid on the Duncan news release, Rhoda had made a few long-distance phone calls.

Maureen Kittering, Duncan's secretary, had been placed under protective custody by Special Branch. It didn't take a genius to figure out what was coming down. And Rhoda Carlisle considered herself a genius.

There was no sense waiting now, even for Koo Ling's intelligence. She would return to her flat, pick up Christie and what they had, and go right to the office and file the story.

Suddenly, a small black sedan wheeled out from a

cross street and accelerated at an angle heading straight for the MG.

"Bloody idiot!" Rhoda cried.

She fought the steering wheel, trying desperately to get out of the way.

It was too late to do anything. The other car crunched into the front fender of the MG and Rhoda jammed on the brake pedal. The sports car jerked to a stop. Rhoda swore as she switched off the ignition.

The other car stopped directly in front of her. A man came out of the back seat at once and walked quickly toward her. He wore a dark, rumpled suit and his face was full of remorse.

He leaned inside her window, so closely she could smell his breath. " I am so sorry, madam. I did not see you."

"Didn't see me?" Rhoda cried. "You bloody idiot—"

Her words were cut off by a painful jab in her side. She looked down. The man's arm had moved inside the window. In his hand was a small-caliber automatic, its barrel boring into her ribs.

"You will come with me now, Miss Carlisle."

"What the hell . . ."

"Quietly, Miss Carlisle, no fuss. Step from the car and leave the keys. Do not attempt to run and you will not be hurt." His voice was gentle, yet there was something chilling in the way he spoke. "Please, step out."

"I'll do no such thing!" Rhoda snapped angrily, striving to keep her voice steady despite the cold lump of fear that had risen in her throat. "What do you want?"

"Conversation . . . in the back of our car, there, now."

The barrel of the gun bit painfully into the ribs under her breast. "All right, all right," she murmured.

She opened the door and stepped gingerly from the car. She was barely out of the seat, when a second man emerged from the larger sedan. He dived into the MG, backed it clear, and drove away.

"Car thieves?" Rhoda asked in amazement.

"Not quite. Your car will be returned to you, eventually, if you cooperate. This way."

Feeling helpless, Rhoda let herself be led forward to the other car. The man's grip on her arm was like a steel band.

She was thrust into the rear of the sedan and the man crawled in right behind her. Immediately, the car accelerated.

Rhoda could hardly move. She was sandwiched between the man who had the gun and another Chinese man.

As they slewed through the streets of Hong Kong, the man on her right turned to face her in the seat. His eyes were like black stone and he spoke without moving his lips.

"Miss Carlisle, this morning you visited a man named Koo Ling, to solicit his help in securing some information."

"Who are you? Surely not the police . . ."

The man flipped open a credentials case. "I am an agent of the People's Republic of China, Miss Carlisle, and I assure you I will stop at nothing to make you tell me everything you know."

Christie Greer pulled the sheet from the typewriter, read it over, and dropped it onto the even pile in a small wicker basket.

With a groan, she stood and stretched. She had been writing solidly for the past four hours, moving nothing but her fingers, and her body was telling her about it.

Impulsively, she spread her feet and bent suddenly. Stiff-legged, she touched her knuckles to the floor. She opened her hands, palms flat, and bounced her upper body, stretching muscles and tendons, until her palms touched the floor firmly. The movements were energetic, those of a healthy body kept in top shape.

She glanced at the clock. Rhoda had been gone for three hours. Surely she would be back soon. It was time to get dressed, in case they had to move fast when she returned.

When the shower was adjusted properly, Christie shrugged Rhoda's robe from her shoulders and stepped under the spray.

Instantly her muscles relaxed, letting her brain go to work again.

Rhoda had called. Sir Emery Duncan was dead, an automobile accident. Rhoda was heading for the police station to check it out. When that was done, she would drop by her office and prime her editors that she had a big one.

Christie smiled. She had told Rhoda not to forget to remind her editors that it was a two-woman story.

Rhoda had grunted agreement, and told her that if Koo Ling called to take all the information. She would see Christie in a couple of hours.

Christie dried herself, wrapped her hair in a towel, and dressed. She was just finishing her makeup when the doorbell rang.

She rose from the vanity and moved into the living room. Rhoda had her key. *Who could this be?* Christie wondered. Approaching the door, she was not afraid, just cautious.

She put her mouth close to the doorjamb. "Yes?"

"Missy Carlisle?"

"No, she's not here. I am a friend."

"Cleaning day."

Cleaning? A maid? Christie thought. *Damn.*

"You'll have to come back."

"No can do. Today only."

It was not a male voice speaking in falsetto, nor was it a female voice straining for depth. The voice was innocent.

Some impulse of prudence led Christie to put the chain lock in its long socket before she flicked the latch and pulled the door back. She peered through the three-inch gap.

A heavily built woman stood in the dim light of the corridor. Behind her were two small, slim men in new coveralls. One of the men held a stepladder on his shoulder. The second had four long cardboard cartons of the type that hold fluorescent tubes, holding them like a rifleman at "shoulder arms." Both men were smiling.

"My cousins," the woman explained. "Missy Carlisle say many bulbs burn up. They fix."

"All right," Christie sighed, suppressing her annoyance.

She closed the door enough to free the chain lock, and then swung it wide.

The cleaning woman was huge for a Chinese, taller even than Christie. Her plump shoulders were wide, her bosom enormous. She bent and picked up her bucket. The two cousins followed her into the living room.

The man carrying the fluorescent tubes in the cartons asked, "You know which fixture get new tube, lady?"

Christie gave him a shrug of good-natured helplessness. "I guess you'll just have to try them all." There was a sudden tingle of uneasiness in the back of her mind. Something was wrong.

The cleaning woman had stepped behind her. Christie noticed now the glint of amusement in the eyes of the men she faced. She stared at them, puzzled, not willing to believe she was in trouble.

An arm of surprising strength whipped around her neck, choking her. The cleaning woman's free hand caught her own wrist and the big forearm was pulled cruelly into Christie's throat.

Christie clawed at the arm holding her. Her legs thrashed violently. The arm into which she dug her nails was like no other she had ever felt. It had the soft feel only the female layer of subcutaneous fat can give to flesh, but beneath the softness were layers of cablelike muscle.

She was gasping for air now, struggling to wrench herself free against the overbearing strength and size of the woman who held her. The monstrous breasts against her shoulder blades were soft, but the heavy belly that arched her back was as solid as a beer keg.

The pressure against her throat diminished the flow of blood through her carotid artery. Dizziness engulfed her. The room grew dim. She fought to maintain consciousness, focusing on the faces of the two men, who were smiling in wonder at the strength of the cleaning woman.

Christie barely saw the two men step forward. She kicked out at them with her legs, but they easily avoided her. One of them held her free arm and the other injected her with a hypo.

Whatever the needle contained, it had one hell of a kick. Christie felt all strength leave her body. She was still awake, but she couldn't move.

Above her, voices spoke softly to one another, their tones matter-of-fact, amused.

Inches from her eyes, Christie saw a pair of medium-heeled women's shoes. The feet they held were enormous for a woman. The ankles above them were thick, big-boned.

She fought her fear. *They don't scare me*, she raged silently. A wave of anger at herself swept Christie. Why had she been fool enough to let them in?

She forced herself to draw in a deep, steadying breath. Regrets and recriminations wouldn't help her now. Somehow she had to understand this, know why this was happening to her.

The huge cleaning woman lowered herself clumsily to her knees, thighs bulging under a white skirt. Spatulate fingers on a thick soft hand slid under Christie's cheek and forced her face upward. Christie looked up into a heavy, coarse-featured, middle-aged woman's face. She was struck by its large pores.

"Don't be frighten. You not hurt." It was the deepest female voice Christie had ever heard. "We take you somewhere nice."

Behind the woman, Christie could hear the men's voices, blurred but distinguishable to her befogged brain.

"This must be story."

"Take it, and her purse as well."

There was some movement, and then, "I got elevator. Let's go."

The cleaning woman lifted Christie's shoulders and slid her arm beneath them. Her other arm went beneath Christie's knees. She raised one knee, bracing her foot solidly, then stood effortlessly, holding Christie in her arms.

Helpless to resist, Christie was carried down the dark,

silent corridor to where a yellow light bulb gleamed behind the collapsible gate of the elevator. They rode silently down to the ground level. Christie stared up past the woman's shoulder at the grating top of the elevator cage, the silently unwinding, greasy black cables. Resolutely, she fought back her fear.

The two men in the coveralls went ahead to the metal door that opened out onto the street. After a bit, there was the sound of a car engine. One of the men came back to where the cleaning woman stood stolidly, Christie held easily in her arms.

"Come," he said.

He held the door open with his shoulders, and Christie was carried out into the deserted side street. The second man was at the wheel of a panel truck, its back door hanging open. The cleaning woman moved across the sidewalk to the truck.

They must be Red Chinese, Christie thought as she was placed in the back of the panel truck. *But how did they find me?*

Rhoda.

That bitch.

ELEVEN

The house was big, with stone walls, a red tiled roof, and a lot of overhang. The drive angled to the rear. Carter followed it past a kidney-shaped swimming pool set in the middle of half an acre of lawn.

He parked and walked up a graveled path that crunched underfoot. A line of poles to his left carried a set of heavy cables to a small wing of the house. He supposed the wing would contain Lady Pang's worldwide communications network. It was a network that controlled a fleet of tankers and freighters, one of the biggest commuter airlines in Southeast Asia, and a fleet of fifty fishing junks that supplied her four canneries in as many countries.

All of it was legitimate, as was Lady Pang, now.

Carter had known the woman for years, clear back to the time when she had owned only two ships and nothing they had carried had been legal.

He rang the bell and the door opened.

The girl who opened it was a willowy ash blonde. Her voice had a Scandinavian lilt when she spoke. "You are Mr. Carter?"

"I am. And you are . . . ?"

She shrugged. That was none of his business. "Come in, please."

As Carter entered, he looked her over quickly: good figure showing through wine-colored lounging pajamas, fine bone structure and eyes that were violet-blue.

"This way," she said, closing the door behind them.

He followed her down a narrow corridor into a large room with heavy, dark wood ceiling beams, a fireplace about half the size of a boxcar, and a lot of leather around. The books that filled one wall were leather-bound. The chairs and sofas and even the tables were leather-covered, and there was a faint odor of saddle soap in the air.

"The bar is there. Help yourself. Lady Pang is just finishing her bath."

Carter watched her hips under the pajamas work their way out of the room, and then moved to the bar. He found a bottle of scotch, dropped ice cubes from a leather-covered bucket into a tall glass, and poured a long one.

He made himself comfortable on one side of the fireplace, took a pull at the drink, and waited.

And waited.

"Oh, Nick, I am so sorry to keep you waiting."

He lazily rolled his head around.

The woman standing in the doorway was still beautiful. Ten years ago and twenty-five pounds less, she had been stunning. She was dark, with a mass of disheveled black hair hanging down to her shoulders, classic features, and a sensual, scarlet mouth. Her voluptuous body was partially concealed in a loose robe that she was holding together with one hand. Her feet were bare.

"Crap," Carter replied, but with a smile. He moved across the room and brushed her cheek with his lips.

"You kept me waiting because the only time you see me is when I want a favor."

"You're quite right. Fix me a drink."

By the time he had found and opened a half bottle of chilled champagne, Pi Pang had curled up on the couch with her legs tucked beneath her.

"Cheers," he toasted.

"To money," she replied.

"How much?" Carter asked, sipping his drink.

"I looked at a map of the island, and I've managed to get a sketch of this Sim's villa. Also, my people on Formosa tell me he has dogs and about ten guards. If you get in and have trouble getting out, it will take at least a five-man backup."

Carter shook his head. "No backup beyond a diversion plus transportation."

Her large Eurasian eyes got larger. "What if you can't get out by yourself?"

"I'll just have to."

"Have you a way in?" she asked.

"Yes," he said, nodding. "I have people who will make the contacts for me."

"I don't suppose you'll tell me why you're going after Sim?"

Carter smiled. "Only need to know."

She shrugged and pulled a map from the drawer of a coffee table in front of her. "Hutchins didn't give me a timetable."

"I'll fly over to Taiwan tomorrow afternoon. Give me forty-eight hours to get onto Sim's island."

"Then?"

"Then another twenty-four to do the job."

Lady Pang nodded. "Then you'll want transportation four days from now, midnight."

"That should do it."

She spread out a map of Yatsu Island on the coffee table. For the next hour and a half, they went over every inch of the island's topography, and then over the floor plan of every building. When that was done, they agreed on the equipment Carter would need and how she could get it to him.

At last Carter leaned back. "Sounds good. Now, your price."

"Thirty thousand should do it."

"My employers can manage that. I'll arrange payment tonight. Where?"

"My account in the Hong Kong bank. Gold certificates, please."

Carter chuckled. "Always cautious."

"Always." She scribbled on a pad, tore off the page, and handed it to Carter. "My account number."

He pocketed it as the blonde walked into the room. "Dinner."

Lady Pang glanced at Carter. He looked at his watch. It had been over three hours since he had told Myang two hours. He stood.

"Wish I could. I've got to move."

The blonde disappeared and Lady Pang took his arm. "I'll see you to the door."

"Call Hutchins when you have a contact on Taiwan for the equipment."

"I should be able to arrange everything yet this evening," she said, and then smiled. "You haven't commented on my new playmate."

"Lovely," he said.

"Sure you don't want to stay for dinner?"

He again brushed her cheek with his lips. "Even if I weren't busy, I think I'm not up to it."

Lady Pang laughed out loud. "You are getting old."

"You're so right."

Halfway around the island, he spotted a restaurant with a lounge and pulled into the parking lot. Inside, he bought a drink and downed half of it before he went to the phone.

Hutchins was out. Carter read everything the man needed to know into a tape recorder, and returned to the bar. He was tempted to have one more, but thought better of it and walked back toward his car.

He had just stepped from the tunnel that led from the restaurant to the parking lot, when a voice from the darkness froze him in his tracks.

"Hello, Carter."

The body behind the voice stepped into a pool of light, and Carter felt a ripple run up his back.

"Hello, Kurt."

Kurt Richtor, hit man, originally out of Hamburg but didn't much care where he worked. He was big, mean, ugly, and deadly.

"What brings you to Hong Kong, Kurt?"

"I work out of Macao now. Europe got a little warm and the money's better here."

Carter's eyes flicked to Richtor's right arm. It hung loosely at his side, palm toward the rear.

Carter knew there was a finely balanced stiletto under that sleeve, honed to scalpel sharpness, the point hovering just above Richtor's palm. He also knew that the man could raise that arm faster than the eye could see, and spear a pinpoint at thirty feet.

Ten short paces separated them.

"I'm carrying, Kurt . . . Luger, shoulder rig, left side."

"I figured," came the raspy voice, the tone tinged with a touch of disgust. "Want to try for it?"

Carter knew that would be foolish. The stiletto would be in his throat before he got his right hand across his body.

"No need to. If you wanted me dead you would have stuck me without saying a word."

"That's true. Gentleman wants to talk to you. He's in an American boat, a Cadillac at the dark end of the lot. Want to head that way without trouble?"

Carter knew Kurt Richtor was a bit of a sadist. He truly enjoyed his work. Could he be working for Myang and her father? Had she sent Richtor to fetch him?

"Anybody I know?" Carter asked casually.

Richtor shrugged. "I'm just a hired hand."

"I know that, Kurt. That's all you ever were."

The other man's jaw clenched in a white line. They had met in Berlin the last time, and the hired killer's stiletto had missed. He was no match, physically, for Carter's superior speed, size, and strength. Carter had broken the man's arm in two places.

"You want to start walking now, slow?"

"No."

"I got orders to fetch you or snuff you." The flat face stretched in a grin.

"Is that right?"

"That's right. Why don't you start running?"

"I think you're bluffing, Kurt."

"Oh? How so?"

"I think you're supposed to mess me up and bring me to talk to someone, but not kill me."

Kurt Richtor wasn't too bright and he was a lousy actor. The look on his face told Carter he had hit the right button.

"I'm walking past you now, Kurt. Try and stop me and I'll use the Luger, noise or no noise."

Carter edged past him, turned, and took a few steps. Instantly, he knew he had miscalculated. Richtor didn't take the bluff.

Behind him, only the thudding feet made a sound. Carter drew the Luger, not to fire but to use as a billy club on the other man's skull.

He gauged the intensity of the sound, and did a three-quarter turn. He had guessed wrong. Richtor was too close to club.

Carter dipped.

Something hard and heavy shoved the side of his head just before his shoulder filled the other man's gut. The Killmaster made springs out of his long legs, and Richtor sailed over his back. As he did, he managed to get a good kick to Carter's forearm. The Luger spun away to land beneath a car.

Richtor had improved since the Berlin days. He landed well, rolled, and came back up in a fighting crouch, facing Carter.

Now Carter could see what had nearly scrambled his brains. There was a ten-inch sap in Richtor's right hand.

"You were right, bastard," Richtor hissed, moving forward on the balls of his feet. "The man said bring you in alive. Messed up, okay, but alive enough to talk."

The left arm came up and that hand now sported the stiletto Carter had expected earlier.

"You'll be alive, bastard," the man cackled, "but truly messed up."

"Hand-to-hand, Richtor, I can kill you and you know it."

"I don't think so, not anymore. And I have these. Your toy is under that car."

"I won't piss around, Richtor. I'll kill you."

The sap made a whirring sound in the still air and the

stiletto came up to catch more light. "Don't think so," Richtor hooted.

"Don't, Kurt."

"You haven't seen me work close with this, have you, Carter? I can peel a pear and never touch the flesh."

The instant of real danger, danger Carter could see, hear, and soon touch, made his adrenaline flow. Sweat drenched his armpits and beaded his forehead as he duplicated Richtor's crouch and started moving.

He could go for his own blade bound to his left ankle, but that might make the other man go for a kill.

No, Carter thought, let him think the advantage was all his until the right time presented itself.

He was pretty sure the man wouldn't use the stiletto until he got in close—too much risk of error, fatal error—so he concentrated on the sap.

Richtor kept coming, circling, moving in a soft crouch. Carter went with it until they had reversed and the lights of the restaurant were in Richtor's eyes. Carter moved back until he could feel the rough bricks of the tunnel against his jacket.

"Stupid," Richtor hissed.

"Just scared," Carter chuckled.

Richtor feinted with the stiletto and roundhoused the sap. Carter slipped sideways and the sap grated harmlessly against the wall, showering them both with brick dust.

Levering forward, Carter tried again for the man's gut, this time with a forearm and an elbow. But Richtor recovered quickly and swung the heavy leather-covered lead a second time to thud high on the bone atop Carter's right shoulder.

"Aggg, shit," Carter groaned, and lurched forward, jamming the heel of his hand into Richtor's face. He let his momentum carry him on past Richtor into the open.

"Hurts like hell, doesn't it?"

It did. Bolts of pain shot down Carter's arm to tingle the tips of his fingers as well as create a deadening sensation halfway to the small of his back.

"Who wants to see me, Richtor?"

"You'll see. I'm having too much fun to stop now."

He came on fast, like a bull, but still light on his feet. Both arms were swinging wide and forward.

Again the sap caught Carter, this time in the ribs, only to be followed by the stiletto cleaving his jacket and shirt from armpit to belt, getting a bite of flesh along the way.

"Gonna hammer you, Carter," Richtor bellowed.

"Fuck you," Carter hissed, anger boiling in his gut now.

"Gonna hammer you, cut you, then hammer you some more!"

"You keep at it, Kurt, and I'll kill you for sure. You're lucky I didn't kill you the last time."

Richtor's face was flushed red. Carter was pretty sure that rage was replacing reason. He could sense it from the random way the stiletto was cutting swaths of air closer and closer to his chest.

Carter backpedaled and hit brick again, but this time on two sides. He was in a corner.

Just as he expected, Richtor came upright for leverage and easier access to Carter's face.

Carter slid down the wall onto his butt. At the same time, he knotted his fists together and brought them hard up between Richtor's legs.

The man howled in pain and dropped the stiletto, digging at his crotch with his left hand to assuage the pain.

"Bastard! I'll kill you, bastard!"

"No, Richtor."

Carter came up, then rolled. Still in agony, Richtor dived, bringing the sap down. It grazed Carter's cheek, but the Killmaster now had the other man's blade.

"Give up, Richtor."

"Go to hell!" Richtor roared, swinging again.

Carter rolled into the other man's body, further unbalancing him. The sap hit the stones on the far side of Carter's body, with Richtor's fingers under it.

He let out another howl of pain, released the sap, and tried to roll away. Carter rolled with him and came up on top, straddling Richtor's chest. A handful of hair and a quick yank brought the man's face a foot from Carter's and his throat an inch from the blade.

"Give up, Richtor."

Richtor tried to buck him off, and managed to crawl his hands up over Carter's chest until they found his throat.

"Don't do it, Richtor."

There was no stopping him and he was getting a grip.

"Good night, Kurt."

The stiletto went in just under the chin and up. Richtor was dead before Carter scrambled to his feet.

Behind him he heard laughter as patrons emerged from the restaurant.

A Cadillac, Richtor had said.

But the voices were closer, and there would be all kinds of hell raised when they came on the body.

There was no time to look for the Cadillac and whoever was in it.

Carter felt around for the Luger, found it, and crouched low between the rows of cars, sprinted for the Lotus.

TWELVE

Carter eased the Lotus to a stop under a streetlight and peered into the rearview mirror.

The side of his face was smeared with dirt and his temple streaked with dried blood where the sap had landed. He touched it with a handkerchief, winced, and picked up the car phone.

The switchboard traced Leroy Hutchins.

"I had a problem," Carter said. "His name was Kurt Richtor."

"Was . . . ?"

"That's right. I imagine our island friend put him on me. He used to be out of Hamburg. Try to find out who brought him to Macao or Hong Kong, and when."

"Will do," Hutchins replied. "How did he get on you?"

"That's a good question . . . one hell of a good question. See if you can find an answer."

Carter replaced the phone, hit the key, and the Lotus purred to life. He drove down the hill back the way he had come and onto a small, winding road that ran parallel to the ocean.

He drove with a frown that pulled his brow into a deep vee. The attack stayed with him, unsettling. It had been more than simply unexpected. It had been bizarre, all of it, the timing, the fact that it was Richtor, a killer who knew Carter by sight, and Richtor's obvious instructions not to kill him but to bring him in for some kind of interrogation.

He found the Mews address easily enough, and the villa. It was a medium-sized place, tiered with little cupolas jutting out from the sides. A long circular drive led to the front of the house, but the road he was on continued around the property.

He drove slowly, keeping to the road. At the rear of the villa, thick trees advanced to the edge of the beach from the hillside. He parked and walked through a small gate in the rear wall.

Gently he opened the door of a rear, screened-in porch, crossed to another door, and knocked. No lights came on in the rear of the house, but he could hear the shuffle of slippers through the door.

"Who is it?"

"Your wandering boy," Carter said. "Open up."

"I think you are too late to do any good now," came Myang's hissing reply.

"Don't be bitchy," Carter replied. "I came as soon as I could and I could use a drink."

"There's a bar about a mile down the road."

"You're being hostile," he answered.

"You're being a boor. We are supposed to work together, remember? You almost killed two of my people tonight."

"They were sloppy drivers. Open this damn door. I'm not in the mood to do much more running around tonight."

There was a moment's pause and then he heard the harsh sound of locks being released. The door opened and she was framed in the dim back light. She wore a cream-white robe edged with rust, her dark hair hanging loose around her shoulders. For the first time, he thought, she looked more like a grown woman than a teen-ager.

Her eyes widened when she saw the side of his head. Expressions on Myang's face were quick, subtle things, he had learned, fleeting moments that escaped from her guarded discipline. He caught the sequence of them across her face—surprise, concern, remorse—as she closed the door behind him.

She led him down a hallway and into a warmly furnished sitting room. Books lined the walls, Mozart was on a stereo, and a small bar along one wall was well stocked. She gestured to a chair beside a round table.

"Take your jacket off," she said, moving past him to the rear of the bar.

"Bring a scotch back with you, huh?"

"In a minute."

She returned in moments with a bowl of warm water and a bar towel. He watched the free, fluid movement of her body beneath the robe and guessed she had little or nothing else on. Slipping his jacket off, he sat in the chair, his arms folded across the back of it as she pressed the warm wet cloth gently to his temple.

"What happened?" she asked, waspishness edging her voice.

"I saw a woman named Lady Pi Pang," he replied. "Ouch."

"I have heard of her. Very bad woman. She did this?"

"No, ouch again."

In halting sentences he told her about leaving Lady

Pang's and being jumped by Richtor. He also told her the rest of it.

"He is dead?"

"Very," Carter said.

He felt the dried blood and dirt being loosened and wiped away. Her robe moved, half-opening as she leaned forward to get at the other side of his head. A pair of soft creamy mounds billowed toward his eyes, gloriously inviting. She noticed his look, straightened up, and the robe closed.

"Did anyone see you?" she asked, and he looked up to see her eyes troubled, concern plain behind the cool façade. It surprised him, an unexpected thing.

"No," he replied, pulling himself to his feet and moving to the bar.

"Do you think Sim sent him?"

"It would stand to reason," Carter said, downing two fingers and hitting the glass again.

"But how do they know about you? We have been very careful, all the plans, no one would have known about the meeting between you and my father."

"Unless there's a leak in your organization," Carter said, sliding onto one of the barstools.

Myang's eyes narrowed. "Impossible. It must be one of yours."

"That's possible," Carter replied. "It's being checked out. Now, what was so important that I had to rush over here?"

"We found out how Dr. Sim planned to connect my brother and our government with drug trafficking out of Hong Kong to Great Britain and the United States."

She crossed to a coffee table and came back with two folders.

"A newswoman named Rhoda Carlisle came to one

of our people here in Hong Kong seeking information. He warned us. It seems that another woman, Christine Greer, had come to Carlisle with surface proof of my brother's involvement. It was Greer who conveniently discovered my brother's body. She removed all his identification. That is why the San Francisco police were not able to identify him.''

Carter took the folders. ''What are these?''

''The written story the women planned to release to the wire services, and transcripts of our interrogation of both of the women.''

Carter's head snapped up. ''You interrogated them?''

''Yes,'' Myang replied calmly. ''I had them abducted.''

''You *what*?''

''I had them—''

''I heard you. Are you crazy? You kidnapped two American newspeople?''

''Of course. That story cannot be released.''

''Jesus,'' Carter growled. ''Where are they now?''

''In a clinic not far from here.''

''That's even worse,'' Carter said in disgust.

''It's quite safe. We own it. It's for the wealthy, offering rehabilitation for substance abuse. It has been very useful for intelligence gathering while they undergo treatment.''

Her calmness at what she had done rattled Carter, but he managed to keep his anger in check. ''We'll have to make a deal.''

''What?''

''A deal,'' he repeated. ''We'll have to make a deal with them.''

''What kind of deal?''

"Trade them the real story if they hold off publishing this one." He waved one of the folders.

Myang thought this over silently and finally nodded. "All right. But until it's all over we keep them in the clinic."

Carter was about to object, then realized that she was probably right. "Okay. Get some clothes on. Let's go see them."

"Who are you?"

"My name is Nick Carter." He crossed the room and flipped open his credentials case. "I'm with a special unit of the State Department."

"The kidnap unit?" she hissed, and mashed out the cigarette she had been puffing wildly but not inhaling.

"Not exactly," Carter replied dryly. "My apologies for what has happened to you and your friend. It couldn't be helped."

"The hell you say. Where is Rhoda?"

"On another floor. I'm afraid she tried to use a pair of scissors on one of the attendants."

"Good for her."

"She had to be sedated."

"Where am I and what the hell is going on?"

Carter took a deep breath and dived in. "I'm afraid you have stumbled onto something that involves national security."

"I sure have," she barked, her voice going up a full two octaves. "The question is, *whose* national security? Does our State Department work for the Red Chinese now?"

Carter passed a hand over his eyes. "In a way, yes, we do."

That quieted her for a moment. "What?"

"Miss Greer, you were meant to find the body of Yang Lee Yong. You were also fed clues to Yong's involvement in the smuggling of drugs. But drugs play only a minor part in it all."

"I'm listening. Who supposedly steered me in this direction?"

"A man by the name of Sim, Dr. Chiang Sim."

For the next half hour, Carter laid out Sim's plan to her. He held nothing back, in the hope that she would realize that the story he was offering her was better than the one she already had.

By the time he finished, an inscrutable smile crinkled her green eyes. "So you're going to waltz onto this Yatsu Island, get Sim's files, and botch up his grand plan?"

Carter nodded. "That's the idea."

"And what happens to Sim?"

Carter hesitated. "I won't know that until the time comes." He couldn't very well tell a civilian that, if he could, he planned on terminating the good doctor.

Christie stood and began to pace. Carter lit a cigarette, watched her, and waited. He couldn't help but think that even in the sacklike hospital gown, gaping slightly open in the rear, that she was a lot of woman.

She was indeed a large woman, but the beautiful proportions of her body were in perfect relation to her size. Added to that was a face that could get you run over turning around to look at again, plus the striking hair that hung in soft waves well below her broad shoulders. A color, he found himself thinking with amusement, that would probably match exactly the downy cushion he pictured between her lithe, golden thighs.

Christie paused in her pacing and turned to face him. "You're going to do all this by yourself?"

"Pretty much so," he said, nodding slowly.

"From the appearance of your head and face," she said, looking him over critically, "you should take some lessons in the art of self-defense."

Carter didn't bother with a reply. He only smiled.

"Yeah," she continued, "I should see the other guy, right?"

He stood. "Do we have a deal?"

"What happens to me while you go off to this island and play cowboy?"

"You stay here."

"No way."

He shrugged. "I'm afraid it has to be that way."

Suddenly she was a dervish. She spun, lightning fast. One kick caught him in the ribs; a second hit dead center in his gut.

The breath whistled out of his lungs and he hit the wall. He gasped but no air would come. Suddenly she was on him, moving with incredible speed. When she was a few feet from him she leaped into the air, spreading her arms and legs wide toward him, clamping them around him as their bodies thudded together.

"Ha!"

It was a yell of triumph, for now she had the hold she wanted. Her long legs wrapped around him, gripping his hips in a parody of sex, her feet interlocked behind him. Supporting their combined weight was as much as he could manage, and for a moment his coolness deserted him and he began to flail punches at her, but because she was molding herself so tightly to him he could get no power into the blows.

She ignored the fists, stretching her arms out on either side of his head and interlocking the fingers as she pulled inward. Realization of what she was going to do made him renew the struggle with added intensity.

This lady wasn't fooling around. She knew the pressure points that would put him out, and she meant to use them.

Strength was draining from him every second. Stars began to shoot across his vision as his tortured lungs labored in vain. Another few moments and he would be on his knees, then on his back.

His groping fingers closed in her hair and he tried to drag her head back, desperate for anything that would give him a moment to draw in fresh breath.

Her weight was forcing him backward, but he made one last blind effort, staggering a step forward, then flinging himself down. As her back crashed to the floor, she let out her breath in a grunt, her grip loosening for a split second. It was enough.

Carter gulped in air and even as he did so, he buried his fist, wrist deep, in her belly.

Christie was sagging but trying to rise when an enormous Chinese woman and two orderlies burst into the room. In no time they had Christie on the bed and the big Chinese woman was giving her an injection. When it was done, she turned to face Carter with a smile.

"She very tough lady."

"Yeah," Carter said, running a hand over his side to make sure his ribs were still whole. "Very tough. Keep her sedated."

The big woman nodded and Carter hit the hall. Myang was waiting for him.

"What happened to you?"

"Never mind. Let's go back to your place. I'll stay there tonight. I don't want to run around in the Lotus if they have it spotted."

She followed him to her car. "I've been thinking about

that. If Sim knows about you, why even go to Taipei? Why not go right to Yatsu Island?''

"Because I want to show myself enough so that Sim's people think I'm still running around on Taiwan when I hit Yatsu. Understand?''

Myang blinked and then shook her head. "Inscrutable, you Caucasians.''

THIRTEEN

"What are you going to do?"

"Clear my head," Carter replied.

"What?"

"A swim . . . you know, the ocean, splash, splash."

He flapped his arms as he went through the rear door and walked swiftly to the beach. He scattered his clothes on the sand and, when he reached the surf, dived in nude.

The water was fine. He took his bearings from an outcropping of jagged rocks and swam easily for about ten minutes, going straight out from the shore. When he checked the rocks he had not veered much.

He lay on his back and rode the swells.

It was the lesser of two evils, keeping the Greer and Carlisle women on ice. Trusting them to stick to their part of the bargain when Sim was eliminated would be a gamble, but one that had to be taken.

He had phoned Lady Pang when they had returned from the clinic, and told her about Richtor.

"Very bad," she had replied. "I suggest a change of plan."

125

"I thought you would," Carter had growled. "Like what?"

"Sim will now know you are coming. I suggest you follow through up to a point."

"What point?"

"Go in, make your connection. Make him believe you haven't guessed, then drop out of sight."

"And . . . ?"

"And you go in from my yacht, the *Sea Goddess*."

"A commando operation won't give me much time in the villa."

Lady Pang had laughed. "If your time in the villa is under lock and key, you won't do any good anyway."

"Too true. I'll let your Taiwan connection know when I want to disappear."

"I'll be waiting."

It would be ten times more risky, and with a thirty-percent-less chance of success, but now it was the only way.

Next he had called Hutchins.

"MI5 and Special Branch in London had agreed to keep a lid on it all until they get the word. They don't want to ruffle the Chinese feathers any more than they have to."

"Any truth in what the Greer woman has?" Carter had asked.

"From the looks of it, lots. It's only old Yong's word against what's on paper that his son wasn't up to his ass in the dope trade. I'm afraid that unless you get proof from Sim otherwise, there's not a hell of a lot more we can do to keep it suppressed."

"I'll get it," Carter had promised, and hung up.

The tide had brought him back in. He touched bottom

with the water up to his chest and started to walk toward the beach.

"Is it warm?"

She stood at the edge of the water, her feet wide apart. She still wore the light-colored blouse and black skirt, but she had kicked off her shoes. The water went in and churned around her ankles, burying them as it slipped back.

"Not bad," Carter replied.

"I have talked to my father."

"Oh?"

"He thinks you are a very brave man and you shouldn't do this thing alone."

"What does he suggest?"

"That I go in with you."

He was still twenty yards out and she spoke quietly, but he had no trouble hearing her over the surf. Her voice was deep now and throaty, and her tone seemed almost amused.

"I don't think that would be wise," Carter said. "Once I'm on that island, I won't have time to stop for petty arguments."

Suddenly she was laughing. She walked forward a few short steps, so that the water swirled around her calves. "I give you my word I will do exactly as you say at all times."

She had edged forward even more now. When it swelled inward, the water was almost to the level of her skirt hem.

Suddenly her hands were at her blouse. She unbuttoned it and pulled it over her head. She threw it backward onto the sand and her skirt quickly followed.

She dived and surfaced with her face inches from his. "Hello."

Her hair was plastered to her head and her eyes sparkled. Carter could see her small breasts bobbing along the surface of the water. She found his hands and pressed them against her until he could feel the nipples hardening in his palms.

"Truce?" she murmured.

"You tried this once before."

"This time is different."

"It is?" he said, feeling the rest of her body move against him.

"Yes. I now know my father was right. If anyone can do this, you can."

Her mood changed again. She laughed, a rich, husky laugh that had nothing false about it. He started to slip his hands around her waist. She splashed water into his face and slipped away, diving under so he saw the flash of her arched back just beneath the surface and then the gleam of her legs.

She surfaced ten yards from him and swam outward. She did a crawl well, moving with sharp, clean strokes and heading off at an angle against the current. Carter watched her for a minute and then went in and walked back up the beach to where his clothes were.

He was smoking when she came out. Her own things were scattered along the sand and she stood there at the edge of the water for a long minute before she started to put them on, brushing sand and water from her body and bending over to wring out her hair.

She didn't look at Carter, but she didn't turn away, either. She had a lovely body, with nice legs and good hips and breasts that were high and round when she turned in profile.

That was when it happened. She was standing there with her legs wide apart and her back half toward Carter, and she was wearing nothing but her panties. The line of her thighs was turned beautifully and Carter watched it as she moved.

She wrung out her hair again, but did it by leaning backward this time, arching her body the way a diver might at the height of a back dive and holding it that way with her arms lifted back and all of her being fluid and lovely in the moonlight. Carter felt tightening along his jaw.

He tossed the cigarette, crawled to where she stood, and pulled her down to the sand.

He kissed her, long and hard. Her lips parted willingly and his tongue did wild things fighting hers.

He was slightly dizzy from the fragrance of her, the salty scent of her, the soft curves of her delicate body pressed against his hardness.

"You know what?" she whispered.

"What?"

"We're both layered with sand. This is going to be very uncomfortable."

"Shower?" he said.

"Shower," she agreed, and they both sprinted for the house.

The shower stall was small, but neither of them minded the crowded conditions. Warm water hissed down on them and plastered their hair against their heads. Carter soaped Myang's body for her, his elbows pinned to his sides. She slipped and squirmed against him.

"We'd have a little more room if you put your arms around me," she told him. "Yes . . . oh, that's better . . ." She leaned against him.

Carter forgot all about his arm and his other aches and pains. She was small and alive and warm in his arms.

Her teeth sank into his lower lip and her thighs clamped him and held him.

"Ah, Nick . . ." Her breath came hard and fast and rose to a whimper. Something snapped inside Carter and he let all the wariness and tightness drain out of him, so that he too breathed hard and fast.

He carried her from the shower and deposited her, soaking wet, onto the bed, caressing her nakedness. Her breast was pliantly firm in his palm. He leaned forward, opening his mouth, and she thrust her breast into it.

He fell onto the bed with her, his lips soft on her softness, and he felt her hands pulling at him, feeling for him, then his naked flesh against her.

"Oh, oh . . . yes, oh, yes," she cried out as his hands found her, held her, moving gently with her.

Her body began to rise and fall in little arches, her legs stiffening and loosening with each quick, compulsive movement. His hands held her, moved expertly against her and she cried out again and clutched him to her.

"Yes, oh, please!" she called to him, quivering and shuddering as though there was nothing else in the world. . Her hunger was more than just wanting. It was an emptying of herself of all the craving that had been locked away, building, gathering.

He turned to cover her with his body, and then slowly moved into her. She cried out with a gasping moan that rose from somewhere deep inside her. There was release and hunger and conquest in it.

He moved gently, slowly, and with each movement Myang sang out and cried again and again and held him so tightly it seemed she tried to fuse their flesh together.

Her body arched under his and she flung herself against him as he moved more quickly. She made small fists with her hands and pounded against his muscled back.

Suddenly she spasmed, screaming into his chest, half laughing, half crying, lifting him in midair and hanging there as time stopped.

She fell back finally, and he stayed inside her until she moved her legs, letting him go. She turned to press her breasts first into his chest, then moving up to press them into his face. He caressed one with his lips and she sighed contentedly.

They lay together, quietly, without words, and slowly she began to quiver again, come alive in stages and move her hands up and down his body. He lay still, letting the wild wanting generate itself again in her until she was moving her lips across his skin, pressing herself on him with little sounds and gasps. And then he took her again and she stayed with him longer until finally she exploded again.

Later she stirred and sat up, her high, round breasts demanding to be fondled. He cupped one in each hand and kissed them gently. She purred like a contented kitten, then pulled away and slipped from the bed.

"I'll be right back."

"Don't go far," he chuckled.

She padded to the bathroom. Carter remained on his back, eyes closed and stretched out in nude comfort. He listened to the muted sound of water running and then heard her pad back into the room. He heard her mixing drinks. When he opened his eyes, she was standing over him, a full glass in each hand.

She hadn't slipped into anything. She remained beautifully naked and apparently planned to stay that way. She stood in the light of the only lamp burning, smiling down at him, the jet-black pubic hair glistening with moisture.

Carter was just reaching for his drink, when the phone rang. Myang stared at it but didn't move.

"Something wrong?"

"It's the scrambler line. A call at this time in the morning . . . it could be problems."

Carter picked the receiver from its cradle and handed it to her. Then he took his drink and headed for the bathroom.

He was just stepping from the shower when Myang appeared in the doorway. "It was my father."

Carter sighed. "He wants to call it off?"

"No, quite the opposite," she replied. "Our people have broken one of the suspects we picked up weeks ago."

"One of Sim's people?"

She nodded. "He told them a great deal about Sim's organizational ladder on the mainland. And something else . . ."

"Yes?"

"His relay contact through Hong Kong to their central headquarters. He was a Korean-American, in your consulate. A man named Kwon Ki."

Carter's breath hissed through his teeth. "That," he growled, "answers one hell of a lot of questions."

He headed for the phone to roust Leroy Hutchins.

FOURTEEN

Christie Greer calmed her muscles and forced her breathing to stay shallow, feigning sleep as the monster-woman rolled through the door. Christie had decided that the woman who had played cleaning lady really was a nurse.

The woman crossed to the bed.

Christie closed her eyes all the way, just in time, as the nurse thumbed her eyelid to look at the pupil. By that time Christie had rolled her eyeballs back in their sockets, the pupils dilated. The nurse gave a little grunt of approval.

When she dared open an eye slightly, the nurse was standing by the side of the bed, adjusting a syringe. She put a hand on Christie's hip; apparently she intended to give the injection in the buttock.

The nurse heaved. She was bent over Christie, just about where Christie wanted her.

All right, bitch, Christie thought, *two can play at the same game. It's payback time!*

Christie whipped her legs high and spread them. When they came down, one leg was wrapped tightly around the big nurse's throat. Christie locked the foot of that leg around her other ankle and squeezed with all the power in her long, muscular legs.

It was too quick for anything other than a strangled squawk from the woman. She fought out of instinct, but there wasn't enough blood to her brain to keep her from blacking out fast.

Christie tiptoed naked to the door and risked a peek. The nurse's cart was outside, a tray of syringes on it. No one was in sight. She pulled the cart inside and shut the door.

In seconds she stripped off the nurse's white dress and pulled it over her own head. It hung like a tent. The big woman's thick black hair was coiled in a knot at the back of her head. Christie worked at it and found several bobby pins. These she used to tuck the dress in so it would look a little less ridiculous.

The crepe-soled shoes were also too large by about two sizes, but tissues stuffed in the toes helped her from looking like a duck when she walked.

She checked the closet: empty. The drawers in the small bureau were also empty.

"Shit, shit, shit," Christie hissed under her breath, and moved to the bedside stand.

There she struck gold, her purse. From it she took her money, credentials case, and her passport. She stuffed everything into the pockets of the uniform.

She lifted a tray of syringes and ampules from the cart and cracked the door. She could hear night sounds, but the corridor was empty. Holding the tray in front of her, she slipped into the hall. She walked quickly, her head held high as if she were in a hurry.

There was a soft pink light in the corridor. It was a

help. The occasional slipper-shod Chinese she passed didn't even glance at her.

There was a guard at the branch of the corridor, a towering shaven-headed Mongol. He stepped out to challenge her.

Christie didn't slow down; that would have been fatal. She looked up and smiled at him. Hesitation showed in his posture. Acting self-assured was a kind of magical passport; Christie knew the guard was thinking that she probably had a right to be there.

He opened his mouth to question her, and Christie dropped the tray. She made herself look dismayed, and stared helplessly at the scattered ampules. He bent over to help her pick them up.

She hit him twice behind the right ear and he dropped to the floor. She dragged him into a nearby closet, shut the door, and snapped on the light.

Quickly she went through his pockets until she found a set of keys. They belonged to a Toyota. All she could do was pray that every car in the lot wasn't a Toyota.

Again the corridor was clear.

The next guard didn't try to stop her. He waved her on impatiently. Christie smiled at him and went on past.

There were no stairs. A corkscrew ramp wound around a central well instead. She looked down the well. There was a little nighttime traffic on the ramp—slow-moving servants, a nurse pushing a man in a wheelchair.

Was this the way out? She had to take a chance.

She was dizzy, out of breath from the accumulation of drugs that had been pumped into her. She gulped great lungfuls of oxygen and prayed that her strength would hold out a while longer.

She walked briskly down the ramp, carrying the tray, a preoccupied expression on her face. The nurse pushing the wheelchair looked up as she passed. Christie nodded and plowed on. Eventually someone was going to wake up and wonder when they had hired a blond-haired, green-eyed nurse.

The nurse passed with a shrug.

Christie went through what looked like a lounge. Two orderlies stood by a door with an Exit sign above it. They were talking and smoking.

Christie detoured to a pair of French doors on the other side of the room, and sailed through them into a moonlit Chinese garden. Crickets chirped and the stars were clear and bright above. The wall and the main gate were across the garden, fifty feet away.

She melted into the shadows, then flattened herself down behind some plantings. The aromatic essence of flowering ginseng came to her nostrils. She was standing beside a low border of smooth, perfectly round stones about the size of grapefruits.

She could see a guard standing in front of the pagoda-roofed booth by the gate. He was a squat, chunky man in blue pajamas and cap.

She drained one of the ampules into a syringe and, holding it by her side, headed right for him.

When he saw her he looked perplexed, then curious, then wary.

Christie walked directly up to him, smiling, her arms opened wide. Before he knew it she was kissing him furiously and grinding her body against him.

By the time he felt the residual sting of the needle in the side of his neck, he was already slumping to the ground.

There were only about twenty cars in the lot. The door of the third Toyota opened with the key.

"All right, Carter, you bastard," Christie said aloud

as she pulled onto the coast road that would take her around Hong Kong, "when I find you, just try and lose me!"

It was a small house off Jordon Road on the Kowloon side. The dark sedan pulled to a stop two blocks away and the driver killed the lights and engine.

The driver was one of Hutchins's people. The man in the passenger seat was head of consulate security. Carter and Hutchins sat in the rear.

"Sure you want to do it this way?" Hutchins asked.

"It's the only way," Carter replied. "And of course none of you know anything about it. Right?"

The consulate man turned to face Carter. "Of course not. We just arrived to question him about some rumors. Wouldn't want to fuck up his civil rights."

"Right." Carter opened the door, but Hutchins's hand on his arm stopped him briefly.

"What if you have to kill him?"

"No chance," Carter said. "He'll crack and give me what I want. You just make sure that he leaks the word to Sim that I've blown him and he's on the run. We topple a few people around the good doctor and he'll make a mistake."

Carter slid from the car and, in shadows, moved to the mouth of an alley that ran behind Ki's house. It was easy to find from the rear. It was the only one on the block with lights burning. A call from the consulate a half hour before saying that he was needed and a car and driver would be sent had taken care of that.

Carter crouched for a full minute beneath the kitchen window. He watched Ki pour a cup of coffee and walk back into the living room. Down a long hall, Carter watched him stop at a mirror to knot his tie.

Carter went swiftly around the house and onto the front step. Ki shouldn't expect anything.

He touched the door buzzer and heard the rattle of a cup on a saucer. Holding the Luger against his side, Carter waited until Ki came to the door and asked without opening it, "Yes?"

Mumbling, Carter said something that sounded like, "Consulate, Mr. Ki, your car."

The lock turned and the door opened slightly.

Carter hit him a glancing blow with the barrel of the Luger, shoved the door wider with a shoulder, and followed inside to hit him again. Ki was tougher than he looked; he stayed on his feet as Carter heeled the door shut.

But not for long. He went down when the pistol broke his collarbone. But he didn't cry out. He didn't scream for help or mercy. He just lay on the carpeted floor with his left arm hanging funny and looked up at Carter.

"Yell," Carter growled. "Go ahead and yell, Ki . . . so I can blow off your kneecaps. Before I kill you, that is."

Ki lay still and closed his eyes. He said nothing, so Carter picked up the cigar smoldering in an ashtray, found another cigar on the table, and lighted it. Ki lay still. Carter puffed on the fresh cigar, got its end cherry red. With the Luger in his belt, he took both cigars to Ki and squatted close.

"Ki, you're a son of a bitch. I should just blow you apart and get on with my work."

"I don't know what you are talking about. You are assaulting an official—"

Carter backhanded him across the face. "Don't give me that shit. To continue. You've got information I can use, shorten my time on the job. You give, you live. It's as simple as that.''

Ki remained composed, lying there, his eyes closed, concentrating the pain away. "You wouldn't dare kill me."

"Maybe not," Carter said, his voice quiet. "But I won't hesitate to take you apart gut by gut, bone by bone. I'll keep you alive, but you'll pray for me to let you die. I intend to start off by stuffing these cigars into your ears, Ki . . . all the way down. You won't pull them out because I'm going to break that other collarbone, and you won't scream because my fist is going to be halfway down your throat. I'll give the cigars time to burn out, and then we'll be ready for the next step."

Ki swallowed. His eyes flickered open and returned Carter's stare. Now his voice was raspy, sandpapered by fear. "I know very little."

Carter moved the cigars closer. "How long have you worked for Sim?"

"From the beginning, thirteen years. He put me through school, then used his influence to get me into the foreign service."

"Then you know one hell of a lot."

Ki's cheeks were pale, shiny with a film of sweat. "Sim has people everywhere. Can you protect me?"

"Right up to the gates of Leavenworth," Carter said. "From there, you're on your own."

"I'll tell you everything I know. Just let me go. Give me twenty-four hours head start."

Carter seemed to think about this. "Sim can still get you."

Ki smiled. "Not if you get him first."

Again Carter seemed to mull it over. "Okay, you got a deal. Tell me about Erica Gruber."

"She was a plant. She let it be known she handled dope shipments for Sim. Yong romanced her and she acted like she went for him in a big way."

"She suckered him in," Carter said.

Ki nodded. "In a big way. She put him in contact with Sir Emery Duncan. Sim wanted to get rid of Duncan anyway. This was an excuse as well as a useful way to do it."

"But the Gruber woman stayed loyal to Sim."

"Like me, she's been working for him for years. He recruited her out of a terrorist group in Germany. She's a fanatic, revolution for revolution's sake. She loves it."

"Where is she now, on the island?"

"Sim set her up in a villa on Grass Mountain, north of Taipei. When she's not working she usually stays there. It's called Sunrise."

"You're doing good, Ki," Carter hissed, pulling the other man to his feet and dragging him across the room to a desk. He slammed him into a chair and shoved a pen in his hand. "I want a list, all the main people who work for or do business with Sim on Taiwan."

"There are several."

"Just the big ones, the ones it would hurt him most to lose."

Ki wrote for a solid fifteen minutes. Carter wouldn't need all the names, but with such a list he could pick and choose.

"Okay," Carter said, folding the paper and putting it in his pocket. "Now I want a layout of Sim's part of Yatsu Island, especially the villa and his offices."

The reply was immediate. "Impossible."

"How so?"

"I've never been on the island."

"What?" Carter couldn't believe it.

"I swear it. I've never been there. Only a few have, top people who have access to Sim himself."

Carter thought for a moment. "Like Erica Gruber?"

"Yeah, yeah, she would know the layout."

Carter backed up and grabbed the phone. Quickly he dialed and the phone in the waiting black sedan was picked up at once.

"Yeah?"

"I got everything I can use from him," Carter said. "Come and get him."

The Killmaster dropped the phone back on the cradle as Ki came to his feet, his face flushed and his eyes grown wide with rage.

"You bastard! We had a deal!"

"I don't make deals," Carter said.

Ki went for him. Carter waited for the perfect instant, and kicked him in the belly. Ki screamed and doubled over, gagging. Carter waited until he was able to straighten up. He hooked a right to the nose and followed up with a left that mashed the tight-lipped mouth. There was blood on his knuckles. Ki stumbled backward, fell against the desk, and slid to the floor. Carter began to use his feet. Kidneys, ribs, groin, face. The blood stained his shoes.

By the time the other three men came in the front door, Carter had already left by the rear exit.

FIFTEEN

The noon flight from Hong Kong to Taipai boarded right on time. Carter had only a flight bag, which he stowed under his seat.

"A cocktail, Mr. Miller?"

Carter leered openly at her breasts where they strained against her uniform blouse. "That's why I fly first class, baby doll, so I can get the first one before I get off the ground."

She tried to smile as she brought the drink.

As the plane rose into the cloudless sky, Carter introduced himself to his seat companion, an elderly Chinese man. "Miller, Red Miller, California. I'm in ready-to-wear. You?"

The man grimaced, grunted something about not speaking English, and studied the sky outside the window.

For the next hour Carter told jokes to anyone who would listen, accenting them with loud belly laughs. By the time the Singapore Airlines flight was on the ground at Chiang Kai-Shek Airport at Taoyuan, he was generally loathed by one and all in the first-class section.

He had noisily drunk three bourbons, made a clumsy pass at the girl across the aisle, badgered the flight attendant for her Hong Kong number, and alienated everyone within earshot.

It was all part of the game. He had spotted two possible watchers at boarding. He wanted to make sure they made sure of him. Because of Ki, Dr. Sim knew he was coming. Carter wanted to announce his arrival with some fanfare. Being overly obnoxious was an excellent way.

Deplaning, Carter was even worse. He complained about the food, the service, the airline, Asians, and the Far East in general. He patted the flight attendant's bottom. Then he belched. Finally, he announced to all and sundry that he'd be at the Grand Hotel, where he would stand any and all Americans who cared to meet him for a drink.

There were no takers. But there was something in the cold eyes and the weathered face that discouraged any manly remonstration on the part of the male passengers.

To top everything off, Carter elbowed two young women out of the way to pirate the first taxi. In the back seat, ordering the driver in a loud voice to take him to the Grand Hotel, he dissolved in laughter. It was going to be fun to be as boorish as he'd always considered so many of his countrymen to be.

It was early afternoon by the time he checked in with the phony passport. He had nailed the two watchers. They had followed him at a distance all the way from the airport in a second taxi. Now one lounged at the newsstand, while the second tried to be inconspicuous looking like an idiot loitering outside on the sidewalk.

Carter turned to the clerk. "I'll need a car, right away."

"Yes, sir, we have a service in the hotel. I'll have one brought around immediately."

In the room, Carter changed into a sport shirt and a lightweight pair of slacks. He had no hardware; the Luger and his stiletto had been left in Hong Kong. It would have been far too dangerous to try and slip them through customs.

The lack of tools would be taken care of—he hoped— by Lady Pang's Taipei contact.

Ready, he hit the lobby. The clerk was efficient: a black, four-door Sentra was waiting for Carter at the curb.

Sim's people, in a white Toyota, fell in behind him as soon as he pulled into traffic. At the first light, a big Honda motorcycle pulled up close.

The rider was a woman in black leather and a helmet with the dark visor pulled down over her face. She revved and turned toward Carter as if she wanted a drag from the light. But when Carter pulled away slowly, she backed off and slid in behind him. Farther on, she moved back even farther into traffic.

She could be a backup for the two goons in the Toyota, he thought, but he doubted it.

He headed west, out of the city into the hills. As soon as he was well away from the more congested area, he deliberately picked a small street that looked completely deserted, and followed it a half mile. Then he pretended to be having engine trouble, and pulled to the side of the road.

He got out and lifted the hood. Out of the corner of his eye as he put head and shoulders under the hood, he saw the Toyota pull into sight and stop.

So, he thought, *they don't care if I know. Now they'll just wait for the right time and place.*

"Fine and dandy," he mumbled aloud, and climbed back into the car.

Lady Pang's man in Taipei, Cholly Wong, lived in the Li Shan district. It was a modern high-rise apartment house on a pleasant, tree-lined street. Carter parked and entered the lobby. He took the elevator to the seventh floor and walked on up to twelve. Sim's watchers wouldn't be able to pinpoint Cholly Wong's flat. One hundred and forty tenants lived in the building.

Carter rang the bell and a lumpy woman in an apron opened the door. Her black hair was drawn back in a loose, untidy bun. She had a petulant mouth and a shrewish glint that spoiled her otherwise pretty eyes.

"I'm Carter."

She nodded and stepped aside. Carter entered and took the armchair she gestured toward.

The woman disappeared into the bowels of the apartment, and a minute later Cholly Wong appeared. He was a dapper little man with dark, restless eyes and receding black hair that had been slicked down with greasy kid stuff. He was neatly dressed, complete with a necktie.

Carter didn't bother with amenities. "I was followed."

"You used some evasion?" Wong asked.

Carter nodded.

"Then it will be no problem. I use one of the bedrooms for an office. This way."

Carter followed him into a cluttered room with two desks, a computer setup, and walls lined with file cabinets. On one of the desks was an open briefcase.

"The things you requested."

In the briefcase Carter found a 9mm Beretta pistol, an Ingram rifle broken down with five loaded clips, four

ready wads of plastic explosive and detonators, and three
incendiary grenades.

"To your satisfaction?"

"Completely," Carter replied.

"Good. Lady Pang explained. Who will you be going
after?"

"Su Pi, the German, Alfred Werner, and the Gruber
woman."

Wong sat at a computer and poked keys. After about
five minutes, he began to talk.

"Su Pi is Sim's most trusted courier. He has a house
near the beach, but he is rarely there. He keeps two
mistresses here in the city. Here are their addresses. All
of his contacts are made out of the Club Nexus."

"I'll try that first," Carter said. "What about the German?"

"The heroin processing plant is in the south. Werner
stays there all the time. Here is a map and the layout.
The Gruber woman is currently in residence at her villa.
Here is that layout."

Carter put the various papers into the briefcase and
closed the lid. Wong motioned him to a map of the island
on the wall.

"Lady Pang will meet you at midnight tomorrow night
in this cove above Keelung. Will you have your business
here done by then?"

"I'll have to," Carter replied.

"Would you like me to have the people following you
removed?"

"No," Carter said. "I would rather they tried for me.
If I do it myself, it will make a greater impression on
Sim."

The Chinaman bowed slightly. "As you wish."

Carter left the building the same way he had entered, via both the stairs and the elevator.

The Toyota was still there, and so was the woman on the motorcycle.

The Club Nexus was in a back alley area off Chung-shan, between Minchauan Road and Mintsu Road. If it was for sale, it could be bought in this area.

Anyone familiar with neighborhood bars in the shab-bier sections of any city in the world would have found the interior of the Club Nexus a reasonable replica of others he had known. The lighting was so dim that Carter had to stand a moment after he had closed the door to see anything at all.

As his eyes became accustomed to the darkness, he saw that there were no tables, just a row of high-backed booths along the right-hand wall and a straight bar, curved some at the near end, on the left. Only one booth, halfway down, was occupied. He could see nearly all of the woman facing him, a tired-looking brunette who didn't even bother to look up as he entered. Her com-panion remained unseen behind the high seat back.

At the far end was a painted blonde, the color of her complexion sufficiently dusky to indicate the blatant ar-tificiality of the hairdo. At the moment she had company, a man on either side, both hunched slightly toward her, their faces featureless in the semidarkness.

The barman detached himself from the trio and ap-proached Carter. He was a burly Chinese of indetermi-nate age, not tall, but strong-looking, his puffy face expressionless, the round head almost completely bald. Not asking what Carter wanted, he waited for his cus-tomer to state his preference.

"Whiskey."

When the drink came, Carter said, "I've been told that Su Pi stops by evenings when he's in town."

"Some evenings."

"Usually from eight to nine?"

"Sometimes."

"But not tonight?"

Nothing changed in the bored, unfriendly eyes. "Haven't seen him," the barman said, and went away.

Carter tasted his drink and put it down. With time on his hands, he did some mental calculation and decided four, maybe five of these would make the sort of drink he was accustomed to. He threw some paper money onto the bar and sauntered back out the door.

Outside in the cool night air, he turned right. He had taken just three steps when they came at him. They must have been waiting right there in the mouth of the alley, the two of them. Carter spun to meet the charge.

Right away he knew they were hired help, not pros.

They didn't split up or circle but came head on, the bigger man a step or two in advance and, foolishly, head down like a linebacker trying to bring down a halfback.

Carter's sidestep was automatic, and as the fellow's charge took him past, Carter chopped hard at the back of the lowered neck. The momentum and the blow sent the man sprawling facedown, and now Carter took a punch on a hunched shoulder, stepped close, and hooked hard with his left.

It was a good punch, well timed, the leverage expertly applied, and the man sat down. That left the second man, and Carter saw the glisten of reflected light on the knife blade. There was no room or time to counterattack, but by spinning slightly he was able to grab the wrist and, still ducking and swiveling, get his back to the man and bring the knife hand over one shoulder.

For long seconds they matched strength, the man struggling to free that hand and Carter bringing up his other hand to strengthen his grip. At the same time he was trying to get his hip into the other's belly. He realized he could do nothing about the man he had slugged because he was on his feet and circling to get behind him. Then he heard the yell.

It was only one simple word: "Hey!"

It was loud, that word, and startled and somehow joyful. Even better, it had a strictly American cadence.

Out of the corner of his eye, Carter saw the leather-clad woman who had been on the Honda. But he had no time to worry about her. He was being besieged by the man with the knife.

He was never really sure what went on behind him. He could hear grunts and a soft continual cursing and the sound of blows. He pulled harder on the knife hand, now well extended over his shoulder, the thin-honed blade in plain sight now as he braced himself and heaved with hips and buttocks.

This time he had the leverage and position, and the man, his feet jerked from the ground, flipped neatly over Carter's shoulder. He struck the paving flat on his back, the shock loosening his grip so that the knife came free in Carter's hand.

It was all over when he turned to see that the first man lay on the ground with his head twisted at a grotesque angle.

The woman was removing the helmet she wore.

Carter groaned as Christie Greer smiled and moved toward him.

SIXTEEN

Carter drove recklessly but with a sure hand. Most people, under the conditions, would be wide-eyed and white-faced.

Christie Greer was calm. She was placidly inhaling and exhaling a cigarette and looking generally bored.

"If you'd tell me where we're going, I could be helping you with a city map," she murmured.

"I know where I'm going," Carter replied testily.

"Then why are you making so many turns?"

"To throw off another tail. You said there was a third man with those two. That means they'll have people all over the city looking for this car."

"Then pull in there."

"Where?"

"That underground garage," she pointed, and crawled over the seat. In a second she was out of sight on the rear floorboard.

Carter could guess what Christie had in mind. She was a headstrong woman, but she knew the angles and she could take care of herself. That was pretty obvious in the way she had escaped from the clinic, got herself a visa, and waited to spot him at the airport. It was also in her favor that he hadn't even spotted her on the plane.

He whipped into the underground garage, got a ticket from the attendant, and went down two levels.

"You sure you know how to do this?" he asked, sliding from the car.

"Honey, I came from a rough neighborhood," Christie answered with a grin. "All my boyfriends boosted cars. Without 'em, I wouldn't go out with the creeps."

"Get something with some muscle," Carter growled, and headed for the exit.

"Will do, dear," she called after him. "Turn right when you hit the street."

Ten minutes and seven blocks away, she pulled up beside him in a nearly new two-door BMW.

"Will this do?"

"Fine," Carter said. "Slide over."

She hissed and spit a little, but she slid over to the passenger seat. "What more do I get to do?"

"Nothing," Carter said, pulling away from the curb.

"Does that mean you're letting me come along for the ride?"

Carter glanced over and gave her a hard stare. "The ride only. Stay out of the way."

"Fair enough," she chirped in a way that had started to get on his nerves.

Ten minutes later, he parked across from a blinking neon sign that read Shinju Palace.

"What's this?"

"A restaurant."

"I'm not hungry."

"We're not looking for food. C'mon, you might make yourself useful."

He circled the building and paused at the foot of some wooden steps leading to the second floor.

"Sim's major courier is Su Pi. His main mistress lives up there."

"And Su Pi is up there?"

"If he isn't, she'll know where he is. You stay down here, over there in the shadows would be good. Back me up if any of his friends happen along."

Christie smiled. "You trust me to do that?"

"Oh, yeah," he said. "I've seen you take care of yourself, remember?"

She faded into the shadows and Carter mounted the stairs. Through a door at the top he entered a hallway. There was a closed door at the end, with yellow light shining from beneath it. He halted and knocked.

A growling voice answered in Chinese. Carter didn't reply and knocked again.

Footsteps, the door opened, and a portly man in pajamas and robe stood in the harsh light.

Carter hit the door and the man at the same time, throwing the door wide open and the man to the floor. The man tried to pull a gun from the pocket of his robe, but Carter was too fast. His foot tramped down hard on the man's gun hand.

There was a yelp of pain, and Carter freed the weapon from pain-weakened fingers.

"Su Pi?"

"What do you think you're doing!"

Carter kicked him in the side. "Are you Su Pi?"

"Yes," the man gasped, trying to hold his cracked ribs together with both arms.

"Where's the woman?"

"Downstairs, getting food. Who are you?"

"Carter. Dr. Sim may not have gotten word to you about me yet."

Su Pi's face changed. The eyes told Carter that he had indeed been informed. He stood warily, rubbing his aching side with his good hand. "It seems we did not properly estimate the danger you represent, Mr. Carter. I suggest you leave here now and leave the country as soon as possible."

"No way," Carter snapped, "I want to meet with Dr. Sim, here in Taipei."

"Impossible!" the man croaked. "No, ridiculous!"

Su Pi telegraphed his move. Carter was ready when the man dived for him.

Carter lifted a short right that caught the other man square on the jaw. He shuddered in midair, fell, and slid across the floor.

Carter towered above him. "I don't know how you contact Sim, but I want you to do it tonight."

Su Pi wasn't through. The man's eyes gave him away.

Carter moved his leg just as Su Pi shot out a foot to catch him behind the heel. Su Pi whirled and half leaped, half dived at Carter's legs. Instead of pulling back, Carter stepped forward, bringing up his knee to catch his attacker along the side of the jaw. Su Pi's eyes glazed and he toppled to his side on the floor. Carter bent over, lifted the man by the robe, and shook him. The man's eyes began to regain alertness.

"You're only making it hard on yourself," Carter said solicitously.

The eyes held his for a few seconds, and then Carter felt the man's muscles tightening. Su Pi's arm came around in an arc, grabbing for Carter's neck. Carter ducked, twisted away, and the man found his feet and whirled just in time to take a pistonlike blow that crashed into his cheekbone. It split the skin and blood spurted.

"Make this easy for me, friend," Carter growled, "or I start using this on your head." He waved Su Pi's own gun in front of his face.

Su Pi slid away against the wall, defeat and a touch of fear in his eyes now.

"That's better," Carter said. "Tell Sim I'll be at the Grand Hotel. Call first. I'll stay there for three days. If I don't hear from him, then I go to him and it won't be pretty. You got that?"

A nod.

Carter went down the hallway and on down the stairs. At the corner of the building, Christie Greer fell into step beside him.

"Well?"

"Very cooperative fellow."

"You've got blood on your knuckles."

"He took some convincing. You drive."

"Where to?"

"South. We're going to cost Dr. Sim some money."

First light was seeping through the covered windows of the laboratory when Alfred Werner finished the long night's work. He removed the rubber apron with fingers trembling from weariness, and examined the last batch of white powder on a large glass tray.

It was the highest quality.

Alfred Werner processed nothing but the highest-quality heroin.

He was a small man with a pointy grayish beard and a muscular figure he kept fit with a couple of hours of bicycling most days. But he was fifty-seven, and right now he looked and felt older. His eyes were bloodshot and the flesh under them was puffy and dark. He had a splitting headache from inhaling too long the fumes from the acetic acid and hydrochloric acid he'd used in the process of transforming the base morphine into pure heroin. And he was exhausted from almost three days and nights of painstakingly detailed work with only short snatches of sleep.

But as he trudged out of the laboratory he had created with Sim's money, Werner consoled himself with the reminder that these temporary discomforts were worth it. He was rich, by his standards, and was going to become richer. Which would not have been the case if he'd remained a small-town druggist in Cologne.

Outside the old mud-brick farmhouse, he paused to fill his lungs with the cool fresh air and dig some aspirin from his pocket. He made his way to the well between the two houses. Popping the tablets into his mouth, he drew up the bucket, dipped in the ladle, and washed them down.

One of the two gunmen Sim had hired to guard the lab emerged from the smaller of the two houses.

''Is it ready?''

Werner nodded, and instantly squeezed his eyes almost shut at the stabs of pain that radiated behind them. ''All done and ready.''

''Good''

The gunman went inside the house to wake the other guard. Werner again inhaled deeply a few times, then turned toward the larger house he shared with his wife, Elsa.

''You want something to eat?'' she said as Werner entered.

''Later. Wake me in an hour.''

He entered the dim bedroom and flung himself across

the bed, too tired to take off more than his shoes. Within
seconds he plunged into a deep sleep.

Approaching the crest, Christie pushed the accelerator
to the floor. When she had enough speed built up, she
switched off the engine and coasted over the top of the
hill.

"Is that it?"

"That's it," Carter replied. "Pull over about halfway
down."

She did as he asked and they both spilled from the car
to stare down at the three buildings of the small farm.

"It looks like any other farm around here . . . no fence,
no walls."

"That's the idea," Carter muttered, checking the plastique and detonators, and squirreling them away in pockets. "There are two guards, armed to the teeth. What
have you got on under that rig?"

Without a word, Christie peeled off the boots, riding
jacket, and the leather pants. She stood in a braless halter
and a pair of skimpy white shorts.

"That should do it. Give me a half hour before you
come down."

Leaving her, Carter made his way off the road and
down the slope in an arc that would bring him up on the
rear of the farm buildings. He went over two low fences
and in twenty minutes, keeping the terrain between himself and the farm buildings, he was sitting in a grove of
trees one hundred yards away.

He used another five minutes to orient himself and
spot everyone's position as best he could.

One guard, a big lumpy man with a shotgun slung
over his shoulder, sat in the shade of a tree in front of
the lab building. The second one lounged on the porch

of the house, sipping coffee. He had an AK-47 across his knees and a big-caliber revolver in a shoulder rig under his armpit.

The first one, in front of the lab, was the problem. He had a commanding view of the driveway in front, as well as the open ground between Carter and the rear of the houses.

Through the rear window of the larger house Carter could see movement. It was the wife.

Where was Werner? In the lab? The house?

He settled down to wait.

Exactly five minutes later, he heard the sound of the BMW's engine and then saw the car coming up the lane.

Both guards responded by moving out of sight. The wife moved into another part of the house. Still no Werner.

Christie Greer's long, bare legs slid from the car. She stood and moved around to the front where she posed, hipshot, cleavage gleaming above the skimpy halter.

"Anyone here who speaks English?" she called. "I think I'm lost. Could someone direct me back to the Yan Lo highway?"

The lab guard, without his shotgun, moved into the yard toward the car. Werner appeared on the porch of the larger house wiping sleep from his eyes. He, too, moved toward the BMW. The wife stayed on the porch behind him, an automatic in her right hand held out of sight behind her leg.

Carter gambled that guard number two's attention was entirely on the confab in front of the BMW. He sprinted across the open space and silently slid through the open rear door of the house into a small kitchen.

He could see the second guard crouched on the floor by a window in the front room. The AK was up and ready and he was paying attention to nothing but Christie.

Now everything hinged on them believing her tale of
being lost. Carter couldn't hear the conversation, but
evidently they did.

Christie got back in the BMW and idled down the
lane. The guard returned to the lab. Werner went back
to the house and his wife followed him inside.

Carter made his move. He padded across the room
like a cat. In one swift movement he got a handful of
the man's hair and jerked his head back. At the same
time, he ground the barrel of the Beretta up one nostril.

"One sound, just one, and your brains decorate the
ceiling. Understand?"

"*Ding ma*," came the angry but quick reply.

"Good," Carter continued in Chinese. "Set the AK
down carefully, quietly. Good boy. Now, with two fingers pull the magnum and set it on the floor."

When this was done, Carter moved the snout of the
Beretta behind the man's ear. With his free hand he felt
for and found the long-barreled .44 magnum. He hefted
it and spoke again.

"What's your friend's name?"

"Wa."

"It better be. I want you to call old Wa over here.
Tell him the fresh coffee is ready. Got that?"

"Yes."

"You'd better. My Chinese isn't the best but it's good
enough. Tell old Wa anything else and you're dead where
you stand."

The man stood at the window with both guns in the
small of his back. He called out. Wa answered. Carter
was satisfied with the exchange.

He chanced a quick glance out the window. Wa was

heading for the house, the shotgun slung, barrel down, over his shoulder.

Carter laid the barrel of the .44 against the man's head just behind the ear with a sharp crack and caught him before he hit the floor. He dragged him into the kitchen and returned to stand behind the door.

Wa came through the door without a pause. The .44 was slightly off the mark on the first blow. The barrel hit too low. It broke a collarbone instead of Wa's skull. He bleated in pain, staggered, but didn't go down.

He whirled on Carter, trying to unsling the shotgun. It was halfway up when a second blow with the long barrel caved in the front of his skull.

By the time he hit the floor Carter was at the window, checking the other house. He waited a full minute. When neither the wife nor Werner emerged, he moved out himself.

He made one complete loop around the house. He couldn't see, but he could hear the woman in the bedroom. Werner was at the kitchen table forking food into his mouth.

He was halfway to his feet when Carter came through the rear door. He stepped forward and rapped the man's head with the butt of the Beretta. It was a stunning blow only, but Werner slumped back in the chair.

Carter turned. The bedroom door was slowly opening. He crossed the room in three long strides, grasped the doorknob, yanked the door wide, and shoved his gun forward into the face of a woman of about forty. At the same time, his left hand swept down and knocked the small gun out of her grasp.

He seized her by one arm, pulled her into the room, and kicked the door shut. He propelled her to a chair close by the unconscious man and flung her into it. She was looking at Werner with horror.

"He's alive," Carter said. "How long he'll stay that way is up to him."

She glared at him. She wasn't bad, Carter decided. A little plump, but appealing enough in thin pajamas and a gossamer-thin robe.

"Wa! Kay Lin!" she suddenly screamed.

"They can't hear you," Carter said. "Old Wa is dead, and his buddy's sleeping."

"Why do you do this? What do you want?" she cried.

"I want you to carry a tale of woe to Sim," Carter said, kicking Werner's ankles. The pain snapped Werner awake. "When does the next shipment go out?"

The woman compressed her lips and her face grew stormy with anger. Carter kicked the man's foot again and when he groaned, he grasped him by the hair, pulled his head up, and got him back in the chair so that he was sitting erect.

"I asked you a question," he said.

"Go to hell," the man replied.

Carter shrugged. He pulled the sash cord free of the man's robe, grabbed him again, and twisted him around. He pinned his wrists behind his back, all the time keeping an eye on his wife. Using the cord, he tied the man's arms tightly and then dragged him to his feet before he shoved him back into the chair.

"I'll have to kill you," he growled. "I've no other recourse. But I think I'll let you live a little longer. That is, if you don't stir out of the chair and you don't raise your voice above a whisper. Either one of those acts will get you a bullet through the face. You understand, mein Herr?"

Werner didn't answer. Carter then backed to where

the woman sat. He reached down, grasped her wrist, and yanked her to her feet. He drew her to him, facing him, and held her there while she fought off his attempts to kiss her.

Looking over her shoulder, Carter grinned lewdly at Werner. ''Before I do my killing, I like a little fun. You will excuse me, please. For a few minutes. If she is cooperative and nice to me, she will not be harmed.''

Werner tried to rise, but it was impossible with his arms lashed behind him. Carter kept the woman's body tight against his own and forced her toward the bedroom door. She was whimpering now, fighting him less and less because her strength had run out.

''Be back shortly,'' Carter said. ''Stay where you are or I'll kill her, too.''

He pushed the woman into the next room, kicked the door shut, wrapped both arms around her until she gave one half-strangled scream.

''Come on,'' he said loudly. ''You know what this is all about. Don't be so damned bashful . . .''

He hooked a small straight-backed chair with one foot and sent it crashing to the floor. From the other room, Werner gave a moan and then called out clearly.

''Let her go! I will tell you what you wish to know. Let her go, please!''

Carter didn't let go, but he freed one arm, reached for the door, and pulled it open. ''Better hurry up,'' he warned. ''I'm getting to the point where I don't give a damn if you do talk.''

''Let her go and I'll tell you.''

''Tell me first, mein Herr.''

''Noon today, the pickup is at noon today.''

''And where does it go?''

''The Standard Shipping Company warehouse in Tamsui. From there it is transhipped to Hong Kong."

"Where in Hong Kong?"

"Standard's main warehouse. From there I don't know where it goes."

"I do," Carter growled. "How can Sim be implicated?"

"He can't. He never sees the stuff, and the payments are made into several accounts before they get to him."

"Figures," Carter said, dragging the woman back into the room. "Sit, don't move."

He returned to the bedroom and ripped open drawers until he found several pair of pantyhose.

He tied the two of them together back to back, and then secured their legs. Finished, he moved around to face Werner.

"The name is Carter. Nick Carter. Remember it. When the goons come for the pickup, they're going to find ashes. You tell them to tell Sim it was Carter, and if he doesn't meet with me, this is only the beginning."

The Killmaster strolled across the open ground to the laboratory, waving one arm toward the hilltop road where Christie would be waiting.

Inside, he set both plastique charges. The boom wouldn't be a big one, but with all the chemicals in the building, the subsequent fire would reduce everything to nothing.

He checked his watch, 10:30, and set the timers on the detonators for one hour.

Christie was waiting in the BMW, the motor running, when he emerged from the lab.

"Hot damn, my man, I have to say you are one efficient dude."

"I love my work," Carter said, sliding into the passenger seat. "Let's go."

"Where to?"

"There's a private beach at Chinsan, lots of summer homes."

"We're vacationing?"

"We're going to break into one of them and get some rest until dark. From Chinsan, it's only a twenty-minute drive to Grass Mountain."

The BMW roared down the lane and Christie turned north. "May I ask what's at Grass Mountain?"

"Not what, *who*. A woman named Gruber. I think you've heard of her."

"Oh, yes," Christie trilled. "What do we want with her?"

"We're going to kidnap her."

"Goody! Never a dull moment!" She floored the BMW and Carter crawled into the back seat. He was asleep in seconds.

SEVENTEEN

It was off season. They had their choice of several large bungalows, all backing directly onto the beach and private. Carter chose a two-story completely surrounded by trees and a high wall with wrought-iron gates.

The lock on the gate proved no problem, as did the door leading from the garage into a huge, modern kitchen.

Christie went directly to the refrigerator. "There's frozen."

"Go ahead," Carter said. "Just clean up completely after yourself. I'm going to resume sleep."

With Christie at his heels, Carter made for the stairs. He cased both bedrooms. The one on the left had a massive bed with a sculptured wooden back extending halfway up the wall and a footboard that a champion fence climber would have trouble getting over.

"Lovely," Christie said.

"No," Carter replied, moving into the second, rear bedroom, "too neat, with too many things that could be out of place."

The second bedroom was furnished simply, almost

stark, with twin beds. The bath and shower was newer, more modern and easier to clean.

"This one will do," Carter said, stripping to his shorts and stretching out on one of the beds.

"Sure you don't want something to eat?"

"No. Just sleep," he said, and felt himself fading as her bare feet padded down the stairs.

The sound of the shower awakened him. The drapes had been pulled, but from the cracks of soft light at their edges he could tell it was dusk.

Carter slitted his eyes when the bathroom door opened and Christie appeared.

She stood in the doorway drying her hair with a towel, and the only thing she was wearing was a heavy perfume.

For an appreciable time, Carter stared at her, his eyes still hooded, but no longer with sleep. He had seen tall women before, but never one so beautifully, perfectly proportioned: the classic oval face with its high cheekbones, the long column of her neck that disappeared in the flat sternum separating her prominent breasts with their pink medallions and nipples standing out like nailheads.

Her waist was surprisingly slender, flaring out to smoothly rounded hips and long firm thighs. Her flat stomach curved down into a wedge the color of gold that emphasized the ivory tint of her flesh.

She was standing with her feet apart, her hips thrust slightly forward, and her posture was the embodiment of sex.

Sex in a large package.

She smiled. "Are you going to shower?"

"Yeah," he said, standing and peeling off his shorts. "Where did you get the perfume?"

"In there." She nodded toward the bath. "They won't miss a little perfume, will they?"

"Probably not."

"Also, there are some jeans and light sweaters in that chest. May I?"

"Lots?"

"Lots," she nodded. "They'll fit."

"Okay," Carter said, moving past her into the bath, "but nothing else."

He was dressed when she came up from the kitchen with a tuna sandwich. "The kitchen's clean."

She was dressed in a dark knit sweater and a pair of jeans that hugged her hips and thighs like a second skin.

"I thought you said they would fit," Carter chuckled.

"God, you're romantic," Christie groaned, moving to the bathroom. "I'll clean up in here."

A half hour later they were in the car, Carter driving. He spent the twenty-minute drive explaining to Christie her part of the evening's operation.

"You see, I do come in handy," she said when he'd finished.

He shrugged. "I make it a point: use what you have."

He stopped about a half mile from the villa and consulted the map that Cholly Wong had given him. A secondary road that wandered aimlessly across the countryside passed to the rear of the villa. It would mean a long walk across unfamiliar fields. And as it was a cloudy, starless night, it would be slow, difficult walking.

He drove on past the house another half mile and backed the car up a leafy lane until it was hidden from the road.

He placed the briefcase on the hood of the car and opened it, revealing the rifle inside.

"That's an Ingram. Can you use it?"

"If you put it together and load it," Christie told him.

He did, and explained the safety. "Take the briefcase, too, and this." He dropped the Beretta inside and closed the lid.

Christie looked at him, her eyes narrowing. "You're going in there unarmed?"

"That's the whole idea," Carter said. "If Sim thinks la Gruber and her bodyguards have me, he'll send a small army from his island to pick me up."

"And that will mean fewer to handle when you get there."

"That's right." He turned and tossed the keys to the BMW as far as he could into the trees. "We'll be using Gruber's Rolls to meet Lady Pang."

The house was a black silhouette against the dark night sky and not a light was showing. Which didn't mean there weren't lights on downstairs in the shuttered rooms. The iron gates at the entrance to the drive were standing open, and from the weeds grown up around them, they hadn't been closed that year. Carter gave the driveway a wide berth and climbed over the stone wall. Driveways were prime places to install electronic alarms. There were plenty of trees and bushes to provide cover, and when he reached the rear of the villa, Carter was confident that even a guard with night glasses couldn't have spotted him.

The garage had a flat roof joining the back wall of the house about halfway up. By using the ornate stonework, he could climb to the roof and from there reach a second-story window.

He picked the lock on the small door beside the main doors to the former stables, eased it open enough to squeeze through, and closed it behind him.

The Rolls was inside, a convertible with the top down. Carter checked and found the keys in the ignition.

He searched for a ladder and found one lying under a pile of discarded luggage. He took it and propped it against the garage roof.

So far, so good.

There were two servants inside the house, a maid and a housekeeper. He wasn't worried about them. Erica Gruber had two young, husky bodyguards who probably also served as live-in studs. She had that reputation. Those two he was worried about, but only until he got inside the villa.

When he reached the roof, he pulled the ladder up, carried it across, and leaned it against the wall of the house. It reached to within a foot or so of a gabled window.

Luck was with him.

There were no wooden shutters inside, and the window was unlocked. It opened easily, and Carter climbed into a small room under the eaves with the musty smell of many years of disuse.

The door was unlocked and the passage behind it led to a narrow stairwell. Carter took it down to the lighted second floor. He checked the four doors on the floor. Three were bedrooms, one a sitting room, all empty.

Music wafted upward from the great room on the first floor. He followed the sound down the hallway.

He was poised at the head of the stairs when, suddenly, a fifth door—one that Carter hadn't spotted—opened and out stepped a big blond Aryan type. The man uttered a curse when he saw Carter, and a darting hand filled with a Smith & Wesson .38.

Carter's hands shot into the air and he spoke in German. "Peace mission, friend. I want to see Erica Gruber."

The big blond smiled, but there was no humor in it. "Then why didn't you come in the front door?"

Carter shrugged, noting that the hammer on the .38 wasn't cocked. "I didn't think she would see me."

The grin became a leer. "She won't. Down the stairs, there's a room in the cellar waiting for you."

It was too good to be true, and Christie would have only one of the guards to deal with. "I think we should really talk to the lady first."

"Move."

Carter did, down the stairs with the blond behind him, too close behind him.

The Killmaster paused and turned slowly. "Listen . . ."

"Move it!" the big man said, prodding the back of Carter's neck with the gun.

Carter grabbed his gun arm with one hand, spun around, and brought it over his shoulder. He got the other hand on the man's wrist and pulled. The blond had to either come up or risk a broken elbow. He came up, and Carter heaved him over the rail with his shoulder. He went down the stairwell trailing a hoarse scream, hit the bottom landing, and lay very still.

At that moment the door of the great room flew open and a woman stepped into the hall.

Carter calmly moved on down the stairs, lighting a cigarette. "Sorry about that. Erica Gruber?"

"Yes," she said, echoing his calm, and then glanced down at her feet. "Is he dead?"

"Very likely. He looks to have a broken neck."

Carter was three paces from her now, and in one look he could see her usefulness to Sim.

She was beautiful. Big mountain-pool blue eyes and hair the color of corn silk hanging to her shoulders. She was at least six feet tall, and built like a lady wrestler.

She had broad shoulders and an easy grace in her long legs. Her full breasts swelled over the top of a lime green figure-hugging dress chopped just below her crotch.

Even at that, there was nothing about Erica Gruber that promised a cozy cuddle.

"You look like an amusing man," she said, her blue eyes assessing him as if he were a slab of beef.

"Oh, I am, I assure you."

"You're Carter, aren't you."

"I am. Dr. Sim has contacted you?"

She threw back her head and roared with laughter. "Dr. Sim has contacted everyone who works for him now, has ever worked for him, and several who have never worked for him. He wants your head."

"And I want his."

Another laugh, this one more throaty, derisive. "And that's why you come here? Let's have a drink."

"Anything that's scotch and not cheap."

He followed her into the great room and over to the bar. She fixed the drinks with strong, sure hands and passed one over to him. Again the eyes appraised him.

"Just who are you, Carter?"

"I'm bad. Very bad," he said, sipping the scotch.

"Oh, I'm sure of that. What makes you think I would betray Dr. Sim?"

"I'm gambling that before the night is over you're going to be more afraid of me than you are of him."

The calm expression never wavered. "You have a very evil look on your face."

"Congenital deformity."

"Are you armed?"

He lifted his arms. "Not even a machete."

"Good. Claude, if he moves, shoot him . . . many times."

Carter turned around on the barstool. Standing in the doorway was a clone of the blond Carter had thrown over the stairwell, only bigger. He also had a .38, and he handled it as lazily as his partner had.

"I don't plan on doing a thing," Carter said, "but sitting here and enjoying my drink. He really doesn't need that."

"I'll be the judge of that. Excuse me."

Carter watched her glide from the room, and then he turned to the man with a smile. "How's tricks, Claude?"

There was no response.

Carter glanced at his watch. Everything hadn't gone exactly as planned, but then nothing ever did. Christie should be in the house by now. Carter was sure she would compensate.

Five minutes later, Erica Gruber came back into the room. "Sim is sending a team from the island to get you. They should be here in about an hour."

Carter couldn't suppress a wide grin. "A team? Out of curiosity, how many men does Sim use to constitute a team?"

She frowned. "Does it matter?"

"Only to me," Carter quipped. "I like to know what I'm worth . . . you know, how dangerous I am."

She shrugged and rescued her drink from the bar. "Five, perhaps six. If it makes you feel good, the doctor considers you a very dangerous man."

"Bravo and olé," Carter said, grinning broadly, and finished his drink.

She turned to Claude. "Put him in the cellar and get that mess out of the hallway."

Claude nodded and motioned toward the hallway with the barrel of the .38.

Carter slid from the stool, bowed to Erica Gruber, and exited the room. Claude fell in behind him, but didn't make the mistake his mate had made of getting too close.

Claude gave Carter curt directions through a maze of hallways, and they eventually ended up in the kitchen. It was dark.

"Fong . . . Fong!" Claude rasped. "Damn lazy bastard."

"Who's Fong?" Carter asked.

"Cook. There's a light switch near your head, there. Hit it."

Carter hit the switch, and out of nowhere Christie Greer hit Claude.

A sharp chop broke his wrist, sending the .38 skittering across the tiled floor. At the same time, she raised her right knee and snapped her foot back into Claude's shin.

He howled with pain and lurched against the refrigerator, hopping on one foot.

Christie struck again, this time a knee with a satisfying, solid crack. Claude howled again and dropped to the floor. The blow had also spread the big man's legs apart, leaving his groin undefended.

Christie Greer was now operating on instinct, applying the basic techniques of martial arts she had obviously practiced for many years. It was elementary physics: the greater the speed and the more precise the timing, the more damaging the impact. It wasn't unlike the head of a golf club striking the little white balls.

Only in this case it was Claude's balls and the striker was the woman's heel.

Carter winced as Christie spun to her left and snapped her foot again, this time higher, into Claude's crotch.

A strangled, whimpering groan escaped from the back of the big man's throat. He clutched himself and rolled to his side. A blow to the side of his neck finished him.

Christie turned to Carter. "Show-off," he said, and moved to the trapdoor in a corner of the kitchen.

"You outlined the rules," she said with a shrug, and dragged Claude to the opening.

Together they dumped him down the stairs and secured the door.

"Where are the servants?" Carter asked.

"In their quarters."

"Dead?"

"Of course not. I tied them up."

"Just wondering," Carter said. "For the All-American girl reporter, you're getting very bloodthirsty."

"Isn't that why you let me come along?" she replied stonily.

"Touché. This way."

They made their way back to the great room. It was empty. Carter motioned to the stairs and they went up silently.

There was the sound of movement behind the second door. Carter twisted the knob gently. When the door gave, he shoved it open and they both surged into the room, fanning out to each other's flanks.

Erica Gruber stood at the foot of the bed, the dress at her feet. She wore only panties and bra. She was in the motion of unfastening the bra, her pendulous breasts spilling from the cups, when they hit the room.

"Buckle back up, darlin'," Carter said. "We're going for a boat ride."

The *Sea Goddess* was 170 feet of pure luxury. It lay at anchor some two hundred yards out in the dark cove.

Lady Pang herself was at the wheel of the launch that
would take them out to the yacht. Myang Yong, already
in a black wet suit, was aft. The minute everyone was
aboard, she moved to Carter's side.

"What is she doing here?"

"The reporter?"

"Yes."

"Seems your people at the clinic goofed. She made
asses out of them all."

Myang glared but shut up. The bow of the launch
lifted and with a roar they moved away from the slip.
Carter went forward to where Lady Pang stood at the
wheel.

"Got to hand it to you, Nick."

"How's that?"

"No matter where you go, you end up with a harem,"
she teased.

"Look who's talking," he shot back. "Where's your
blonde?"

"Left her at home, of course. I don't like my ladies
to know about my seamier side. Is that Gruber?"

Carter nodded. "I think she knows it's the end. She'll
tell us everything if I make a deal with her."

"And?" she replied, one eyebrow arching.

"And what?"

"Will you make a deal?"

Carter smiled. "I'll tell her I will."

They were aboard only ten minutes when Lady Pang
had the crew hopping and the yacht moving south along
the coastline at eighteen knots.

Fortified with rum-laced coffee, Carter assembled
Myang, Christie, and Erica Gruber in the chart room.

"All right," he said, placing a legal pad and some
pens in front of Gruber, "I want to know how many men

are left on the island. I want to know the layout of the villa, down to every window and door. I want to know Sim's habits when he's in the kind of hot spot I've put him in. And I want to know where all his records are stored.''

Myang Yong leaned forward until her face was only inches from Gruber's. ''And I want to know who killed my brother, and what you had to do with it.''

Gruber momentarily lost her poise, but regained it quickly and faced Carter. ''I have money in Switzerland. If I tell you everything, will you put me ashore in Hong Kong?''

Carter glanced at Myang. She avoided his eyes.

''If nothing happens on the island that is a result of your wrong information, and we get off alive with everything to bury Dr. Sim, I'll have Lady Pang land you in Hong Kong. Beyond that, you're on your own. Agreed?''

There was a long moment of silence, all eyes focused on her as she glared at Carter.

And then Erica Gruber picked up one of the pens and began to write.

EIGHTEEN

"For safety's sake, we're passing nearly a mile from shore," Lady Pang explained. "That should be no problem with the sea sled."

Carter turned to Myang. "Hang on tight. If you slip away I can't stop for you."

Myang nodded and went on adjusting her gear.

Lady Pang continued. "We'll be moving at a steady ten knots with only running lights. Anything less than that and someone on the island might get suspicious."

"Get over the horizon as soon as possible," Carter said, "and don't come back in until you see the villa go up, no matter how much time elapses."

He finished examining his gear. Everything seemed to be in order. The plastique, detonators, and incendiary grenades were strapped to his chest. The Beretta was snug in a waterproof holster rig on his right hip. An eight-inch commando knife was on his left hip. He had swim fins and webbed gloves for his hands. A coil of black nylon line hung from his belt, and he wore a black rubber face mask pushed high on his forehead.

A seaman materialized with a pair of tanks. Another

came forward with tanks for Myang. They helped them into the harness and cinched up the straps. Carter checked the quick-release buckle to make sure it was in the secure position.

By now the yacht had begun to slow down and he knew they would soon be in the water.

At the top of the ladder, Lady Pang rejoined them. "When I drop my arm we'll stall for a few seconds. Be sure to go deep and stay clear of the screws. Once we're past, come up in our wake and get your bearings. You can look for the sled then."

Carter nodded, saw Christie Greer give him a thumbs-up sign, and started down the ladder. Together, he and Myang knelt on the little trailing platform.

Carter slipped the mouthpiece between his teeth and flipped open the regulator. He took a couple of deep breaths. Everything was working well. He pulled the face mask into position and saw Myang do the same.

They crouched with their backs in the water and their necks craned so they could see Lady Pang's arm.

He heard, rather than saw, the sled go.

Lady Pang dropped her arm.

Clamping one hand over the mask, Carter let go of the ladder and tumbled backward into the ocean. As soon as he hit the water he lost his bearings and couldn't tell up from down. He could hear the loud swish of the yacht, and the churning sound of the propellors seemed right on top of him. All he could think of was Lady Pang's warning: "Stay clear of the screws."

He decided to gamble and began swimming in what he hoped was a downward direction. He turned out to be wrong, but his luck held and he broke the surface about thirty feet from the yacht.

He ducked back under immediately and swam into the

turbulence of the yacht's wake. The water boiled and churned around him. Fighting hard, he managed to hold his head out long enough to get his bearings on the sled.

Then he saw Myang's head bobbing less than ten feet away. They nodded to each other and swam to the sled.

In the moonlight he could see the rocky coastline of the island very clearly against the sky.

By the time Carter shifted the sled around to face the island and hit the battery power, Myang had attached herself to his back like a leech.

The little propellor began to turn and the bubbles thrashed back along their bodies. Because the prop was well below the water, turning slowly, it left very little wake.

Carter spent the fifteen minutes of their electric-assisted swim scanning the line of rock against the sky. He saw no movement and no outline that would resemble a man.

But even though Sim's private little army was depleted, Carter knew there would be one—and probably two—sentries patrolling.

Finally the sea sled bumped ashore on the rocks at the foot of the island. Without a signal, Myang rolled from his back and helped him pull the sled from the water. They secured it under an overhang of rocks, and re-examined their equipment.

Myang unslung the Ingram and attached a silencer. Carter peeled away the waterproof covering from the Beretta's holster and pulled the commando knife from its sheath.

"You know the play. Stay fifty yards behind me, pick up anything I miss. We're safe from sensors until we get to the villa itself, but out here is where the sentries will be. Got it?"

Myang nodded grimly. "Let's go."

Carter began the long climb toward the summit. It was slow going, the trip made even more difficult because of the necessity to avoid starting a minor rock slide that would give away their position.

Halfway up, he found a ledge and crouched there for some time. And it was only the thought that going down was possibly even more dangerous than continuing up that spurred him on. Finally he crawled over the top and, well away from the edge of the cliff, lay down in the long grass until his muscles stopped twitching.

Unless Sim had added to the original warning system installation, the thermal detectors were scattered along the ground in front of the villa, facing the cove, as well as on each side. When Carter had studied the plan that Erica Gruber had drawn, he had thought this curious. Or careless. After climbing the cliff, he appreciated why Sim had not thought it necessary to protect his sanctuary from that direction. Carter snaked along the ground, using the bushes and tree trunks to shield himself.

Instinct made him stop and burrow into the grass just as he heard a slight cough. Carefully, he raised his head.

A man was standing not more than six feet away, a pair of night glasses glued to his eyes. He was standing sideways to Carter, looking out to sea.

Slowly, not even breathing, Carter took what seemed an eternity to slither the six feet.

He clamped one strangling arm around the sentry's neck and slid the knife up under the man's ribs with the other hand, sinking the steel deep. Apart from a slight gurgling sound, the man died quietly and before full terror had roused him to desperation.

Carter moved on. There was bound to be one, maybe

two more sentries on this side of the island outside the villa compound.

Two hundred yards across the grassy field, moving from tree to tree and bush to bush, Carter came on another sentry.

This one would be more difficult. Either he was conscientious or nervous, for he kept looking around to see into the darkness behind him, and his pace was uncertain: a second's pause here, three quick paces there.

Carter crouched in the shelter of a bush and cursed silently. Too risky to chance a knife throw. Unless it killed instantaneously, even a feeble cry might rouse the villa.

Carter flexed his fingers. They were tingling with anticipation as he put away the wet dagger and took the nylon cord from his belt, unwinding it from the wooden grips around which it was coiled, wiping his fingers free of blood to give himself a firm grip.

The sentry was on his return trip now, his rifle slung in such a way that to attack from this side would be difficult. The moment he was to die would have to be on the next patrol, when the rifle would be on the side away from the Killmaster.

The attack was smooth, the wire cutting through the neck before the sentry was aware he was finished. Carter put a knee in the man's back and gave the wooden handles a vicious extra tug. The sentry collapsed.

Carter moved forward again. It was nearly a mile when he once more smelled the tang of salt air and knew he had made it all the way across the island.

· Then he saw the villa and his mind went back to Erica Gruber's written description: "It was originally a monastery, very defensible from the sea because it is perched on a rock ledge whose face is almost vertical right down to the ocean. There is a single gate on the landward side. It is guarded by two sentries at all times. Exactly fifty yards from the gatehouse is a low concrete bunker. This houses the generators . . .''

Then he heard it, the only sound breaking the heavy silence: the low-pitched hum of a generator. He was practically standing on the bunker.

It was a matter of seconds before he found the door. It was unlocked.

There were two generators, one shut down. Using a penlight, Carter traced the wires through the wall, and then returned. By size and common sense, he could figure which set served the buried sensors surrounding the compound.

He severed them and went back topside. Myang was waiting, lying on the grassy mound that formed the bunker's roof.

"The sensors?"

"Done," Carter replied. "Any trouble?"

"I added one to your two."

"Get twenty yards to my right. Use your nightscope. Be sure you get both of them before they can give a warning."

She nodded and slithered away. Carter gave her a full minute to get into position, then moved forward.

A narrow lane led up through the trees to the villa. He worked his way across the broken ground until the building was a solid black patch against the night sky.

He crouched behind a bush and studied the huge, wooden gates and the old monestery behind them. There were three floors forming four sides of a large courtyard, with open galleries on each floor. He could see small square openings for windows cut through the thick stone walls on the second and third floors, and a flat roof.

Two large lanterns in wrought-iron buckets hung on each side of the wooden doors. If Carter tried to approach over the open ground, the light from the lanterns would illuminate him as a perfect target. He would be dead in ten steps if either or both of the guards were at their peepholes.

He was just getting up the nerve to make a run, when one of the doors opened. He heard chattering, and two men emerged into the light. They walked to the wall, fumbled at their trousers, and began urinating.

Carter was about to give a signal to Myang, when he heard the softly popping sound of the Ingram.

She could shoot. Only two slugs from the short burst missed their mark and sang off the stone wall. The two sentries dropped without a sound.

As one, Carter and Myang ran forward and through the opening in the huge doors. Carter groaned it shut, dropped the loglike bar in place, and turned.

They were inside.

NINETEEN

Staying in the shadows, they crept down a flight of stone stairs to the top gallery. A series of small doors spaced closely together led into rooms that had obviously been the monks' cells. The doors were painted, the fastenings modern, and the stonework washed. Keeping close to the wall, Carter moved along until he found a door partly open, and glanced inside. There were two iron cots neatly made up and a plain dresser under the window.

Guards' quarters.

If Gruber's memory was correct—and if Carter had estimated right—there should be only two more men left to guard Dr. Sim's precious body.

There were four or five household servants, but Gruber had said they rarely stayed overnight. They all lived like peasants in fishermen's shacks at the very end of the island.

Carter and Myang moved on to the next gallery. There, the ceiling was higher, and as there were fewer doors, the rooms were considerably larger. As far as he could see, all the doors were closed. He continued down the stairs at the end of the gallery.

On the ground floor, Sim had made some major structural alterations. The rough stone of the floor had been tiled with modern tiles, and the doorways into the spacious rooms enlarged with modern plate glass doors installed to provide light, as there were no windows in the outside walls. There was a great deal of wrought iron, including massive four-sided lanterns suspended from the vaulted ceiling of the gallery.

Both of them crouched together in the darkness for a conference.

"According to Gruber, there should be two more," Myang whispered.

"I know," Carter said. "Sim's inner sanctum is through that door. It's steel, and always locked from the inside."

"The plastique?"

"The only way. It will bring everyone running."

"I hope Sim is in front of the pack," Myang said tightly.

"Chances are he's in there, probably monitoring his people in Taipei. Cover me—I'm going to pack the door."

He hurried across the tiles, tugging a small package of plastique and a detonator from the pouch across his chest. As fast as he could, he packed the seam around the door. He set the detonator for two minutes and jammed the spike end into a glob of the explosive putty.

He was wriggling back across the tiles when a guard appeared on the stairs to his right.

The guard spotted Carter, yelled, and raised his automatic rifle. A shot hammered out from somewhere along the middle gallery. The guard fell forward on his

knees, a look of intense surprise on his round face, and
the gun slipped out of his hands. Carter raced down and
swept it up and ducked between two potted oleander
bushes. He scanned the arches along the second gallery
and saw no sign of Myang.

And then things began to happen fast, and Carter forgot
about Myang. Three men ran out of the guardroom by
the gates. One of them stayed there and directed the other
two up to the second gallery. They raced up the stairs,
and when they reached the top, they split.

Carter chose the man running around to the right and
fanned the trigger. Three shots ripped off. The man slid
forward on his face. The guards by the gates sprayed
Carter's position, and the Killmaster flattened out, his
face kissing the tiles.

Although they were shooting wildly, Carter reckoned
it was only a question of time until some of their lead
found him. He poked the Beretta around and emptied
the clip in their direction.

They stopped shooting and scattered for cover. Carter
just had time to reload when the steel door blew. He got
to his knees groggily and rushed the room. Through the
smoke he saw a man wildly rushing toward him. He
wore heavy spectacles and a white lab coat and bran-
dished a heavy-caliber revolver.

Carter shot him in the chest and stepped aside to let
him fall into the hall.

From somewhere in the courtyard there was heavy fire.
Carter turned back into the computer room. He crossed
it and flung open the door of a large, paneled, private
office.

Dr. Chiang Sim sat behind a huge desk, outwardly
calm.

He was fatter than in his photograph, and white-haired

now, but still looked solid and powerful. He stood up, his feet apart, his great fists on his hips, and a scowl on his bloated face.

He was well dressed, in a dove-gray linen suit with a rather showy white silk tie, but he still looked like a peasant, with sturdy shoulders and a thick, muscular neck, and wrists of very creditable solidity. His jacket was open and pushed back over his big belly.

There was no gun visible. With an army around him, he probably never figured it was necessary to carry one.

"I assume you are the American, Carter."

"You assume right."

"It will be very embarrassing for the Americans when I tell the world that they have staged such a brutal attack on my property."

"I doubt it," Carter said, moving forward. "Especially if I have your computer files."

"Never."

"Where are the record tapes and the keys?"

"What do you propose to do when you get them?"

"Kill you."

Carter did a quarter turn. Myang was moving into the doorway, the Ingram leveled.

"Ah," Sim said, still calm, almost smiling, "I have seen your photograph. Very lovely. You are, of course, the sister."

"You killed him."

"Of course I killed him. Your brother became a very greedy man. He also betrayed me when—"

Myang fired a burst and shot Sim's legs from beneath him. The man went to his knees, but he still had guts.

Myang had come too close. Sim reached out and twisted the Ingram away. As it spun from her grasp, Sim swung her in front of him. With his free hand, he pulled an automatic from beneath his belt at the small of his back.

Carter cursed and leaped, too soon. He tried to check his forward motion but saw that he couldn't, and he let his legs collapse as Sim fired.

The shot creased the wet suit at the shoulder and Carter felt the split second heat of it as he hit the floor. He rolled, slamming into Myang's ankles, feeling her go down on top of him. He kicked out as he heard Sim cursing, trying to get a moment for another shot.

Carter got a leg behind the man's leg, yanked, and heard the shot explode, the bullet smashing into the floor just above his head. He pushed himself upward with his hands, kicking out with both legs, catching the man hard in the gut. Sim half-collapsed, and Carter made a forward dive, almost a football tackle, sending Sim down. The man twisted as he hit the floor and tried to bring his arm up for another shot. Carter knocked it backward, coming down with his knee in the man's belly.

Sim gasped and fell backward again, and Carter moved for his gun hand. The man brought his shoulder up hard, and Carter felt it smash into his chest, and he fell to one side.

Sim seized the moment, rolling away, coming up on one knee, the gun in his hand. Carter fired from the floor. He saw the bullets slam into Sim's belly, then his chest, red stains appearing as though he'd been suddenly splattered with paint. Sim sank forward, rolled onto his back, his legs drawn up, and Myang—her scream rending the sudden silence—was atop him.

Carter had never seen such unbridled rage. A small knife appeared in her two hands and before Carter could drag her away she had cut the old man's face to ribbons.

"Jesus, Myang, he's dead."

''I know,'' she rasped, raking him with her wild eyes. ''I just wanted to make sure.''

The master computer tapes and the keys were in a steel vault. Using the plastique would be too risky. Carter searched the villa until he found a heavy-duty acetylene torch.

''What are you going to do?'' Myang asked. It was the first words she had spoken since she had gone into her killing trance.

Carter fitted the regulators and hose, and with a key he turned on the gas. He noticed that the oxygen showed a pressure of 1900 pounds to the square inch, while the acetylene gauge showed only 7 pounds. The acetylene was used only to provide heat, while a thin dagger of pure, hot oxygen pierced the iron or steel. Nor did it melt the steel. It caused it to disintegrate, blowing it away in bright sparks that cooled to brittle flakes of gray rust.

He put his arms into a leather garment that covered arms, chest, and shoulders. He tied on a leather apron and put on a mask, which was in fact a respirator. He pulled on strong leather gloves and picked up the blow-pipe, which was actually an arrangement of three pipes ending in one nozzle which was a rosette of tiny apertures, with one central aperture for the oxygen.

He went on one knee, not in front of the vault but in a position where he could work on it from the side. The blowpipe allowed for this, being turned at a right angle a few inches from the nozzle.

He set an adjustment on the blowpipe, removed one hand from the oxygen cylinder, and brought out his lighter. He flicked it and held it forward. An eight-inch jet of flame shot from the end of the blowpipe.

He started cutting in a straight downward arc to cut the tumbler bars in the center.

The flame began to play on the safe door. It grew hot enough to glow dully. As the glow became brighter, Carter's hand moved to the trigger on the blowpipe.

"It's an old torch," he muttered, more to himself than to her. "Flame wavers."

Twice he cleaned residue from the tip with the commando knife, each time setting it back down by his knee.

He turned the main stream of oxygen on high, and at once the flame changed its nature. Now it was less than three inches long, driven so hard that it looked like a solid light. When he applied the tip of the flame to the vault door, big golden sparks exploded from the point of impact in a shower.

From then on it was a matter of minutes. Carter turned off the flow of gas from the cylinders. The flame popped off, and he pulled off his respirator to reveal a face beet red and streaming with sweat.

"It's through."

"Will the door open now?" she asked.

Carter nodded and groaned. His left shoulder where it had been nicked by Sim's bullet stung like hell.

"Then stand and move away from the door."

Carter turned his head slowly. Myang stood, feet planted wide apart, Sim's automatic held steady in both hands, the muzzle pointed directly at Carter's head.

"Would this have anything to do with what Sim said about your brother getting too greedy?"

"I'm afraid it would. Move."

He stood slowly, as she ordered, his body sideways to her, his right side away. As he did, he palmed the knife by the blade, running it up the back of his arm.

They moved in a circle, about ten feet from each other,

Myang toward the safe, Carter toward the door.

"What is on those tapes, besides Sim's organizational records?"

"Nothing," she replied. "That much of what my father told you was the truth."

"What *didn't* he tell me? What about Sim's comment . . . that your brother got too greedy?"

"I suppose you have the right to know. My brother was weak. He discovered the capitalist way of life and he wanted to pursue it."

"So he became a traitor," Carter said.

"Only partially. As his last duty, he passed the information we needed about Sim to us. Then he informed my father that he was not coming back to China. He planned on taking over the heroin end of Sim's operations as soon as we crushed Sim."

"I see," Carter said, tensing his right arm slightly. "If that came out, it could be very embarrassing for you and your father."

"My father's position is not one of great strength. He would lose a great deal of face."

"So he told you to take the tapes and get rid of me."

"No. He was willing to take the disgrace if the truth about my brother appeared in Sim's records. You see, he is an honorable man."

"But I don't think you are an honorable woman, Myang."

Her almond eyes flashed. "I have my own code of honor. You are an American, my enemy. I shall have little remorse killing you, and even less when your death saves my father."

"Myang, listen. I have no objections to deleting anything about your brother from the tapes before we pass them on."

"No, I'm afraid not. I could never trust you to be silent."

He could see her knuckles turning white as she applied pressure to the trigger.

"Myang, wait. Have you seen many American films?"

His question took her aback, momentarily easing the pressure on the trigger. "Movies? Why do you talk of movies?"

"There was a fine old film. It was called *The Seven Samurai*. In it there was a scene—"

"Enough!"

"There was a scene where two actors faced each other off, one had a gun, the other a knife. The actor with the knife claimed that it was faster than the reactions of the man with the gun . . ."

"You talk foolishness just to make your stay on earth minutes longer."

Again the knuckles grew white.

Carter's arm went forward with the speed of a striking snake.

The slug from the automatic went harmlessly into the ceiling.

The long-bladed knife went into Myang's throat, its force sending her body backward into the still glowing safe door.

Carter stood up from the console and stretched. He had deleted all mention of Yang Lee Yong from the tape, and then made a duplicate.

Lady Pang would see that one copy got to the old man in China. The other copy would be passed to Hutchins in Hong Kong to be sent on to Washington.

For the next hour, he planted the remaining plastique

in strategic locations around the old monastery. Each detonator was set five seconds apart, the first to go in a half-hour's time. Then he gathered the tapes and made a complete round, firing the detonators.

At the gates he threw the incendiary grenades into as many galleries as he could reach.

He was about two hundred yards away when smoke and flame burst through the roof. It would bring Lady Pang.

By the time he reached the rocky shoreline on the opposite side of the island, the *Sea Goddess* was already anchored and the launch was heading toward him.

He was just stepping into it when the plastique went off.

"The girl?" Lady Pang asked.

"She didn't make it," Carter replied.

Christie Greer came on deck and moved to his side, nodding to the packet containing the tapes. "Is my story in there?"

"Some of it," he murmured. "But I don't think you can ever print it."

She frowned and finally just shook her head. "Do you ever keep your word?"

"Hardly ever. It's the nature of the business. I'll make it up to you, though."

"Oh, yeah? How?"

"I'll buy you a few dinners, say, about a month's worth."

"A few dinners?" she yelped. "A few lousy dinners for the story of the year?"

"Like I say, it's a lousy story and probably no one would believe it anyway. And the first dinner will be in London, the second in Paris, the third in Monte Carlo . . ."

Christie put a finger over his lips. "It's a deal. And if you back out on this deal, I'll break your kneecaps."

Nick Carter nodded and curled his arm around her waist.

This deal he would keep.

He knew she could break his kneecaps.